A GERRY ANDERSON PRODUCTION

5 STAR 5 ™

THE DOOMSDAY DEVICE

A GERRY ANDERSON PRODUCTION

THE DOOMSDAY DEVICE

BY RICHARD JAMES

ANDERSON
ENTERTAINMENT

Anderson Entertainment Limited
The Corner House, 2 High Street, Aylesford, Kent, ME20 7BG

First published by Anderson Entertainment in 2023.

www.gerryanderson.com

ISBN: 978-1-914522-48-2

Editorial director: Jamie Anderson
Cover design: Marcus Stamps

Typeset by Rajender Singh Bisht

TABLE OF CONTENTS

FOREWORD

Legendary TV producer Gerry Anderson had many hits, from **Stingray** and **Thunderbirds** to **Space: 1999** and **UFO**, but he had a few misses, too. In 1977, he began raising funds for a movie project, **Five Star Five**. Writer Tony Barwick, known to Gerry from his previous puppet and live action series, produced a script that was subsequently described as 'Gerry Anderson's answer to Star Wars'.

Stages were booked at Pinewood and Bray but, ultimately, the project collapsed when funding fell through. **Five Star Five** was to become a 'lost project', one of the few Gerry Anderson properties never to see the light of day. Until 2021. Gerry's son, Jamie, passed me the script and suggested it might be ripe for novelisation. I agreed at once.

When I had completed it, Jamie suggested I give it a separate title (*John Lovell and the Zargon Threat*), thus leaving the door open to future adventures. It was a smart move. It meant I could build upon and expand the universe as depicted in that first book, delve deeper into the characters and also answer some questions. Namely, just why did the Zargons invade Kestra? No explanation is ever given in the original screenplay but in this second book, *The Doomsday Device*, I am allowed to offer one. I also enjoyed a bit of world building as I delved deeper into Zargon society and, perhaps, provide a reason for their malevolence.

It was a conscious decision to stick to the characters as presented in that first novel, whilst adding some more of my own. I hope that Gerry would feel they were at home in the world he created, and that there's something of the feel of his screenplay in this second book. It's no secret that **Star Wars** was a big inspiration and so, for research purposes of course, I watched all nine of the films. What I think Gerry was aiming for, and what I hope I've brought to *The Doomsday Device*, is a sense of scale, of a story that's set across many light years. The word *epic* is much used, but that is definitely what I was aiming for. I hope I came close.

Oh, and I got to explain just why Lovell and his friends are known as the Five Star Five.

Richard James, 2023

I

HITCHING A RIDE

Gruff sat alone, which was just the way he liked it. The bar was crowded, damp and dark. The air stank of danger. Over at the counter, two Pethran smugglers were haggling over their spoils, their words increasing in volume as they jabbed each other with their long talons. Most of the other customers, like Gruff, were loners. They skulked in alcoves or lurked in corners, their heads low. It was a bar favoured by outlaws and fugitives. If the local law enforcement hadn't been in the pockets of the landlord, Gruff was sure it would have been raided daily.

Sitting in his favourite corner, he nursed a drink in his huge hands, his eyes flicking around the bar, always alert for danger. He had worked out long ago that this table gave him the best view of the room. Every entrance and exit was covered if he sat forward over the table. During a long and turbulent life, Gruff had learned to expect the unexpected. Even his great size was no deterrent to trouble. In fact, there was always someone who, after a few drinks, would see him as a challenge. His enormous frame, jutting jaw and prominent forehead marked him out as a target. Gruff understood. As a child, he had yearned to chop down the tallest tree in the garden, just to prove a point.

He was a long way from home now. How he'd got here, he wasn't entirely sure. Several bad decisions and a lifetime listening to the wrong people had left him unable to chart a steady course. He'd drifted from bad jobs to worse jobs, fallen into debt and got angry. That, of course, had led to more trouble. Gruff sighed. Life had dealt him many interesting hands. A spell in prison had toughened him up, and three marriages had toughened him up some more. He took a glug from his drink to dispel the memory, wincing as the cloudy liquid hit the back of his throat. He shook his head. He only drank the stuff because it was strong and cheap.

Two more, and he wouldn't care any more about any of his wives. Just as he slammed the glass down on the table and wiped his lips, he caught a movement from the corner of his eye. Through the smoke, he was sure he had seen something by the bar; a quick, fluttering movement. Gruff frowned as he looked down at his glass. Maybe he'd had enough already. As he lifted his gaze, he was startled to see an object in the air, right in front of him. Small visual receptors scanned Gruff's face. Robotic ears twitched with excitement. Gruff's lip curled in confusion as he lifted a huge hand to swat it away. The little dog gave a small electronic yelp of alarm, then turned and fled towards the door, its mini thrusters burning brightly.

'You're sure that's him, kid?' John Lovell stood across the street from the bar entrance, his hat pulled down over his eyes against the rain. Beside him stood Jhy, his eyes closed in concentration. Taking a breath to break the psychic connection with his mechanical dog, Jhy snapped his eyes open.

'He's just how he was described to us,' he said. 'And he's at his usual table, opposite the bar beneath a broken light.'

Lovell sighed. 'Okay,' he rasped, 'I guess I'd better get this over with.'

'Nervous?' Clarence chuckled next to him.

Lovell looked down to his chimp companion, sheltering beneath a white umbrella. 'I don't know the meaning of the word.'

'Be careful, sir,' rumbled Rudy. The robot had found respite from the driving rain beneath a tattered awning. Giving him a nod and hooking his thumbs in his belt loops, Lovell stepped into the deluge and sauntered across the road.

'He's aiming for casual,' Clarence sniggered, 'but he's landed on ridiculous.'

'I heard that,' Lovell called back as he turned. 'Why don't you try and make yourselves look less... conspicuous?' He shook his head in exasperation as he studied his companions. A talking chimp holding an umbrella, a young boy reaching out to catch his flying dog and an eight-foot robot with glowing eyes. 'Yeah,' he mumbled, resigned. 'Forget it.'

The road was busy with passing vehicles and Lovell had to dodge between thundering hovertrucks and makeshift rickshaws.

They splashed water up his legs as they whizzed past. A taxi driver slammed on the brakes.

'Hey! Watch where you're walking,' the driver cried from his open window. 'You got eyes, don't ya?'

Lovell tried his best to ignore him as the driver leaned on his horn.

'So much for not drawing attention to himself,' Clarence snickered from the kerb.

Even from the top of the steps, the smoke stung the back of his throat. As he descended to the door, the smells of the street were replaced by the heady fog of tobacco and alcohol. Lovell knocked the rain from the brim of his hat. He had to wait at the entrance for his eyes to grow accustomed to the gloom. It was the perfect opportunity, he guessed, for those inside to size him up. Just as he was about to step into the room, he was surprised by a glancing blow to his shoulder. Two Pethran smugglers were being roughly ejected by the landlord. Still squabbling amongst themselves, the smugglers fell up the steps and into the pouring rain.

'You lookin' for trouble, too?' the landlord snarled at Lovell. He had a wide face and a patch over one eye. Lovell didn't want to know how he'd got it.

'Just here for a drink,' Lovell lied.

The landlord looked him up and down. 'Take a seat,' he sneered. 'The waitress'll be over.' He leaned in with a wink. 'She costs extra.'

Lovell nodded and jammed the stump of a cigar between his teeth. He hated the taste and would never have lit it, but he thought it made him look the part. He would never have told Clarence. Gazing round the bar, he fought to get his bearings. There, just as Jhy said he would be, sat the man that he was after. Lovell swallowed. This guy was huge. Even sitting down, he was the tallest man in the room.

Summoning his courage, Lovell sauntered over to the table beneath the broken lamp. 'Axim Gruff?' he asked.

The hulking figure at the table barely looked up. 'Nope.'

Lovell pulled up a chair. 'A hundred thousand says you are.'

Gruff downed the last of his drink and slammed the glass down on the table. Alerted by the noise, a waitress scooted over to their alcove.

'Hey handsome,' she trilled. 'Fancy a drink?'

Lovell flashed his teeth in the semblance of a smile. 'Sure,' he leered. 'How about a beer?'

'Not you,' the waitress retorted. 'I said *handsome*.' She nodded towards Gruff. Lovell's smile dropped.

'I'll have another Greel,' Gruff sneered. 'My friend here will pay.' Lovell nodded, determined to keep him sweet. 'And for all my drinks today,' the giant concluded.

Lovell gave a nervous smile, conscious of the lightness of his wallet. 'Just a Zinca juice for me,' he said. He wanted to keep a clear head. Lovell watched as the waitress wriggled back to the bar. Looking her up and down, he noticed that her legs tapered down to a set of wheels. He sighed. Once again, he'd been duped by a robot. 'I'm getting too old for this,' he muttered to himself.

'Whatever you want,' Gruff grunted, 'I want the cash first.'

Lovell shook his head. 'You'll get your share when I get what's mine.'

Gruff's eyes narrowed in thought. 'So, whaddya want?'

Lovell looked around and lowered his voice. 'A ride.'

'Don't you have your own?' Gruff was getting the measure of this new customer.

Lovell winced at the memory of his battered B156 Transporter. 'It's in dry dock.' The lies were coming easily now.

'Where do you want to go?'

Lovell leaned forward over the table. 'Asteroid A330.'

Gruff's eyebrows rose on his enormous forehead, almost colliding with his low hairline. 'The Zargon asteroid?' he scoffed. 'That's out of bounds for civilians.'

'I have authorisation,' Lovell bluffed, chewing on his stub of a cigar.

Gruff gave a low cackle. 'If you have authorisation, why are you asking me for a ride?'

Dammit, Lovell thought. *Why didn't I think that through?* 'Look,' he sighed. 'You've got a ship, I have money –'

'*Will have* money,' Gruff corrected him.

'Sure,' Lovell conceded. 'When I get mine, you'll get yours.'

Gruff sat back and stroked his not inconsiderable jaw. 'Do I know you?' he asked, at last.

Lovell rolled his eyes. Since his part in the defeat of the Zargon attack, he had attained a level of notoriety he wasn't completely happy with. For someone used to operating in the shadows, being so well known was a distinct disadvantage. Unable to run his usual business, he had quickly run out of money. It had been one hell of a six months to be a smuggler. Now the dust had settled, he had to collect his reward from the Kestran president. One million credits in gold bars awaited him on the Zargon asteroid. Rudy, the huge robot, had buried them himself, and only he knew their exact location.

'I need a ride for me and my three associates,' Lovell ploughed on, ignoring the question.

'Then my fee just went up,' Gruff snarled. 'By four.'

Four hundred thousand. Lovell felt deflated. He had already promised a quarter share to each of his companions, including Jhy's stupid robot dog. This wasn't going quite how he'd imagined.

'Why me?' Gruff asked, suddenly suspicious.

'Because you're the best,' Lovell replied, quick as a flash. He had long since learned that flattery worked wonders.

'Or the most gullible,' scoffed Gruff.

'Look,' Lovell pleaded, 'I just need a ride. There and back, no questions asked.'

He was interrupted by the reappearance of the waitress. This time, Lovell heard the whirring of servos as she leaned over the table.

'Hey,' she snapped at the old captain. 'The Greel might be cheap, but gawping's extra.' She passed Lovell his Zinca juice and flashed him a warning look.

'Sweet,' Lovell smiled, weakly.

'Okay,' Gruff grumbled as she wheeled away. 'We got a deal?'

Lovell considered his position. He didn't want to give the giant four times what he'd offered, but he guessed he should agree for now. He could always pull a stunt later and leave him with nothing. In fact, it would give him the greatest pleasure.

'Sure,' he smiled.

'Pier two, three hours from now,' Gruff said quickly. 'Bring your friends, Mr Lovell. Tell no one.'

It seemed the conversation was over. Lovell downed his juice and spat the bitter pips to the floor. It was only when he got to the door that he realised he hadn't told Gruff his name. Alarmed, he turned back into the bar, only to find the huge pilot had already disappeared from his table. Lovell gnawed at his lip, angry at himself. Of course, he would tell Clarence that everything had gone just as he had intended. Straightening his hat and treading his cigar into the floor, the old captain climbed the steps. Just as he reached the top stair, he again felt a blow on his shoulder. It was the two Pethran smugglers again, returning from the rain. Lovell's heart skipped a beat. This time, he noticed, they were armed. Suddenly, he heard the fizzing of laser fire behind him. Ducking down, he couldn't help looking round to see the cause of the commotion. The two Pethrans were firing at the landlord behind the bar. Incensed, he had leaned over the counter, but not before reaching for a pulse rifle of his own. The customers dived for cover, some pulling weapons of their own to join the melee. The air was alive with the hissing of lasers. Light fittings fell from the ceiling and great chunks of masonry crashed to the floor. The landlord stood his ground, firing from the hip. Lovell sprinted through the door just as a huge explosion threw him out and onto the road. Dust and glass fell around him as Lovell threw his arms over his head to protect it. When all was quiet, he looked up to see Clarence, Jhy and Rudy staring at him, their eyes wide.

'Well,' he said with a disarming smile. 'That went well.'

'Did you do the deal?' Clarence asked as he loped through the rain, his knuckles dragging through the puddles on the sidewalk. The bar district was known as one of Estoran's seedier districts. Situated beside the civilian spaceport, it seemed a world away from the gleaming towers and glistening mountains of the capital. Dash, Jhy's little robot dog, had been sent ahead to look for trouble, while Rudy stomped conspicuously behind them, his huge feet sending plumes of water into the road.

'I did *a* deal,' Lovell answered carefully.

'Really, Lovell,' Clarence began, 'I don't know why you're bothering. You've got it good on Kestra.'

'You mean *you've* got it good on Kestra,' Lovell interjected. 'Don't pretend you haven't enjoyed the attention.'

'That's true,' Clarence conceded. His mind flashed to his comfortable new apartment in the capital. Furnished to his exacting specifications, it included sturdy branches to swing from and beer on tap. But Clarence wasn't alone in enjoying the fruits of Kestra. Jhy was back in school, developing his psychic skills and even Rudy had found his place. Free from his bondage to Lovell, he had found employment at the docks, lifting great containers and stacking them onto huge ocean-going ships. Only Lovell had failed to settle into his new life. Something of a celebrity since his thwarting of the Zargon attack, he had toured the vidcast studios and the diplomatic missions. And he had hated it all. Even with Colonel Zana by his side, he had felt awkward, out of place. Clarence noticed how happy he looked now, despite the rain and being blown out of a seedy bar by an enormous explosion.

'You're enjoying this,' the chimp smiled.

Lovell tipped some water from the brim of his hat. 'I'll enjoy it more when I have my gold.'

'Pier two,' Rudy suddenly announced as he lifted a huge hand to point across the road.

'And we're right on time,' added Jhy as he scooped Dash into his arms.

Pier two was one in a row of landing pads for small, civilian craft. Lovell's expression fell as they rounded the corner into the launch bay. An ugly, decrepit ship stood on the pad, steam rising from its aft vents. Cannibalised parts had been bolted onto its exterior and, Lovell noticed, none too carefully at that. It looked like a brick.

'We're gonna fly in that?' Jhy asked, tugging at Lovell's sleeve.

Lovell couldn't imagine it flying anywhere. It looked more like it had been dropped there.

'Hey,' snarked Axim Gruff as he walked down the ramp. 'Beggars can't be choosers.'

Clarence was backing away. 'Oh no,' he was saying, 'you're not getting me on that. Your old freighter was bad enough, but at least it had a certain charm.'

Lovell took a breath. The way he saw it, they had no choice. 'Fine,' he called over his shoulder as he walked towards the craft. 'I'll give your share to the old chimps' home. I'm sure they could do with the bananas.'

The interior was just as chaotic as the outside. Loose cables ran the length of the greasy floor. Unprotected circuitry hung from the walls.

Ducking as he walked, Lovell picked his way carefully through the detritus. 'This is gonna be fun,' he hissed.

'I'm scared,' Jhy admitted.

'Cheer up, kid,' Lovell smiled. 'You got a day off school, didn't you?'

'So, er, where do we, you know, *sit?*' Clarence was looking around the cramped cargo hold.

'You didn't mention you wanted seats,' Gruff scoffed as he folded his great frame into the pilot's chair.

'Of course,' seethed Lovell as he wedged himself into a corner and prepared for lift-off. 'It's always the details that escape me.' He rolled his eyes as Gruff reached up to the propulsion controls.

A chirpy voice cut through the air. 'We hope you enjoy your experience with Astral Tours,' it announced. 'Please, sit back and make yourself comfortable.'

'What the hell?' Lovell exclaimed in surprise.

'The guidance computer's from a tour ship,' Gruff shrugged. 'Listen, I built this ship from scratch. You gotta take your parts where you find 'em.'

Rudy squatted beneath a bulkhead and leaned forward on his hands. 'Come here, Jhy,' he rumbled. 'I will keep you safe.'

Jhy scuttled over the floor to take shelter beneath the robot's great bulk, Dash yapping excitedly beside him.

The ship shook as it heaved uncertainly into the air. Clarence skidded across the hold as it lurched dangerously to one side. In the cockpit, Axim Gruff was wrestling with his dual joystick controls.

'Please tell me you've flown this thing before,' Clarence pleaded as he reached out to grab at a protruding service panel.

'She's a little sluggish today,' grunted Gruff. 'That's all.' He slammed the controls forward as the ship struggled to maintain altitude. Lovell felt his stomach turn as they fell through the air, only to rise again with a rattle of machinery. With no windows to the outside but the cockpit windshield, all he could see was rain slamming into the glass as Gruff lifted the nose skyward.

'To enhance your inflight experience,' chimed the guidance computer, 'hot and cold refreshments will be served soon. We hope you enjoy a comfortable journey.'

'It's as comfortable as a flying brick,' Clarence simpered.

'Happy to let you out here,' Gruff called above the scream of engines, 'but it's quite a drop.'

The chimp screwed his eyes tight shut and decided to concentrate on keeping his breakfast down.

At last, the ship pulled itself above the cloud layer and into the lower reaches of space. Suddenly, all was still. The deafening roar of the engines subsided to a gentle hum and the rattling stopped.

'See?' Gruff leered triumphantly from his chair. 'Even a brick can fly in space.'

Lovell rose from the floor and crossed to stare out the cockpit window. He realised he had been digging his nails into the palms of his hands. 'How long until we reach the asteroid?'

Gruff thumped his nav controls. 'Anywhere between three hours and four days.'

'What?'

'The computer's on the blink,' Gruff shrugged. 'I mostly manage without it.'

Clarence had joined them. 'You fly this heap of bolts on *manual?*'

In response, the chimpanzee felt the barrel of a gun beneath his chin. 'Hey,' Gruff snarled to Lovell. 'You didn't mention what a pain in the butt your friends would be.'

'It's okay,' said Lovell hurriedly. 'He doesn't mean it.' He glared at Clarence. 'Manners were never his strong point.'

'Sure,' said Clarence, raising his hairy hands. His mouth was set into a rictus grin of panic. 'But I'm quick to learn.'

Gruff pushed his gun further into the chimp's neck for effect, then snapped it back in its holster. 'Last passenger who complained,' he hissed, 'found a new home in the asteroid belt. He can just about be seen from the Kestran Space Observatory.'

'Understood,' Clarence nodded. 'Er, Lovell, could I have a word?'

The chimp straightened his tunic and led the way back into the hold.

'The guy's crazy,' he whispered as he leaned against a bulkhead. 'And his ship is unfit to fly.'

17

Lovell looked around. 'Yet, here we are. *Flying*.'

Clarence nodded to where Jhy sat in Rudy's protective embrace. 'You swore to Dorita you'd look after him.'

Lovell blinked. 'In three hours, or four days, or whenever the hell it is, that boy is gonna be the richest kid in the quadrant. And his stupid robot dog.'

Dash gave out a yap of indignation. 'He heard that,' snapped Jhy.

Now the ship was steady, Rudy got to his feet. A whining of servos accompanied every move as he approached his old master.

'We owe you nothing, Lovell,' he began, his great voice seeming to shake the deck plates beneath their feet. 'Which means we are here because we want to be.'

'Sure,' Lovell sneered, 'that and your share of the gold.'

Clarence thought he saw Gruff's ears twitch at the mention of the word. He shot Lovell a warning look.

'I served alongside you,' Rudy continued, 'without promise of payment. I endangered my own life and saw others lose theirs.' The giant robot almost looked sad. 'Somewhere in my memory banks is a file marked *Sumara*,' he said softly. 'It is in his memory that I am determined to do the right thing.' With a groaning of gears, Rudy pulled himself up to his full height. 'I intend to give my share of the gold to the boy.'

Lovell raised his eyebrows. *Sheesh*, he thought to himself. *That kid's gonna be richer than Grassus.*

'Even Grassus had nothing in the end,' Jhy announced to Lovell's alarm. 'He gave it away to the galaxy's poorest planets.' The boy shrugged. 'So says the myth, anyhow.'

'Hey, kid,' Lovell barked. 'Stay outta my mind.' The old captain sighed to himself. Clarence was right. He owed the boy a duty of care. He had promised Dorita. 'Okay, Rudy,' he said at last. 'You got it.' He turned to the boy. Jhy was clutching Dash tight to his chest. 'Just don't spend it all on dog food.'

For the rest of the journey, the little party sat in silence. Clarence watched as Gruff made adjustments to their course. Once or twice, he was sure he saw their strange pilot reaching for the comms panel, only to sit back when he thought he had been spotted. Rudy had found some loose wires on the floor and stripped them. Using it as an opportunity to practise his dexterity, he had twisted the copper strands, tying them together to make a collection of little wire figures. Jhy squealed with delight as the huge robot delicately handed them over. Dash gave a yelp of excitement as he watched his master play, firing his mini thrusters to complete a somersault in the air.

Finally, a harsh alarm sounded from the cockpit. Lovell pushed his hat back on his head and yawned. He looked across the cargo hold to see Clarence glaring at him. Lovell wiped some drool from the side of his mouth. He had clearly fallen asleep.

'We're coming up on the asteroid,' Gruff announced from the pilot's seat.

Lovell and Clarence moved to the cockpit, stretching their aching limbs as they walked. Gruff angled the ship round until a huge rock filled the windshield. Lovell swallowed. It was the first time he had been back in six months.

'If you'd care to look to your left,' chimed the guidance computer cheerfully, 'you will see Asteroid A330, from where the Zargon Empire launched their recent, unsuccessful attack on Kestra.'

They were coming in close now. Lovell could clearly see the remains of the tower of rock that had housed the Zargon fleet. The old captain felt a cold sweat prick at his back. He saw Clarence shiver beside him.

'Prior to its destruction, ten Zargon battle cruisers were housed in the rock below,' the computer continued, 'each equipped with interplanetary ballistic missiles capable of destroying Kestra from outer space.'

As Gruff leaned back on the flight controls, the ship dropped like a stone. Lovell could see there had been changes to the landscape. The site had been almost completely excavated, with most of the rubble deposited over a nearby ridge.

'It has since been purchased for development by Thrills Incorporated, to be developed into a unique theme park and adventure experience.'

Lovell groaned.

'Attractions will include the exclusive Lovell Hotel, a chimpanzee enclosure and a *Rudy the Marauding Robot* ride.'

'Chimpanzee enclosure?' gasped Clarence. 'That's the thanks I get?'

Lovell jabbed his companion in the ribs with a sharp elbow as Axim Gruff narrowed his eyes. 'Sounds great,' Lovell said, breezily. 'Put us down over there.'

'Thank you for flying with Astral Tours, we hope you had a pleasant flight.'

Lovell stepped gingerly onto the asteroid's surface. 'I'll leave a review,' he sneered.

'How long are you gonna be?' Gruff shouted through the open hatch.

'As long as it takes,' Lovell called back. 'No questions asked, remember?'

The first thing he noticed was the scent of the air. It had a sickly, metallic tang.

'They gotta sort out the smell before they open that theme park,' Clarence said as he walked down the ramp.

'They're probably still relying on the Zargon systems,' Lovell breathed. 'I'm amazed they survived at all.'

'Yeah,' said Clarence as he looked at the tower of rock on the horizon. 'Not much else did.' Aside from the remains of the Zargon base, the asteroid looked as bleak and unforgiving as it always had. A grey, featureless terrain stretched out before him. 'How's Rudy gonna know where he buried the gold?' The chimp sighed. 'It all looks the same to me.'

'Coordinates,' boomed Rudy as he barrelled down the ramp. He raised a metal finger to tap his head with an audible *clang*. 'It's all up here.'

'Jhy?' Lovell looked around him for the young boy. 'Send your dog to keep a lookout.'

Jhy nodded. 'Okay,' he smiled. 'Dash?' The robot dog came whizzing from the cargo hold, his tail wagging frantically behind him. 'Run ahead, boy!' Jhy commanded. With an excited yap, Dash whizzed down the ramp and into the barren landscape. 'He'll tell me if he sniffs anything unusual.'

Lovell grunted in response. 'Okay, Rudy,' he grinned. 'Let's go find my gold.'

'*Our* gold,' Clarence corrected him.

'Sure.' Lovell waved the remark away. 'Whatever.'

Rudy bounded ahead, his great feet leaving indents in the powdery dust beneath.

'So, Lovell,' Clarence said as they followed, 'just how much of the gold are you gonna have left by the time you've divided it up?'

'Enough,' Lovell replied, none too convincingly.

'By my reckoning, you've promised a quarter share to me, Rudy, Jhy *and* Dash.' Clarence scratched his chin with a long, hairy finger. 'I hate to break it to you, but four quarters make a whole.'

Lovell sighed. 'I'll take Gruff's share out first. Mine too. You guys can squabble over what's left.'

Clarence rolled his eyes. 'Charmed, I'm sure.'

As the asteroid rolled in space, the perpetual night sky seemed to streak overhead. Every now and then, Lovell spotted Kestra on the horizon. It all seemed a long way away now; the warm nights in the mountains, convivial meals with Colonel Zana. Perhaps he should've forgotten about the gold. Lovell shook his head as he thought. The money would give him something he would never have on Kestra, no matter how comfortable he had become; independence. Besides, he reasoned, he was a wanderer at heart. He'd never been one to settle down, except just that once. Lovell smiled at the memory.

'Looks like he's found it,' announced Jhy.

Lovell lifted his gaze from the dusty ground to see Rudy standing, solid and immovable against the horizon.

'Three five zero by two seven four,' he announced, pointing down to the ground. 'The gold is right beneath me.'

'Great,' called Lovell, impatiently. 'Then get digging!'

'Lovell?' Jhy was tugging at the old captain's sleeve.

'Not now, kid,' Lovell groaned. 'Can't you see we're busy?'

'But –'

'It can wait,' Lovell hissed.

Rudy had bent forward, tensing his arms with a hiss of hydraulics. His eyes glowing, he planted his hands into the ground like shovels and proceeded to dig into the dusty earth. Soon, his arms were a blur. Rudy swayed in a relentless rhythm as he ploughed into the ground, great piles of dirt building around him. His limbs and servos hissed and whined as they were pushed beyond their tolerances. Finally, the robot was standing shoulder deep in a great gouge in the ground.

'It's gone.'

The words hung in the thin air for a moment. Lovell blinked in confusion. 'What?' he gasped, at last.

'Lovell!' Jhy called again.

Lovell ignored the boy, pushing past him to jump into the hole with Rudy. 'How can it be gone?' he shouted, clawing desperately at the ground with his bare hands.

'You're sure this is the place?' Clarence was doing his best to sound calm. 'Perhaps you made a mistake.'

Rudy's huge head swivelled this way and that to confirm his bearings. 'This is the place,' he confirmed.

A roar of engines interrupted Lovell's grief. Looking up, he saw Gruff's ship lifting uncertainly into the black sky.

'Now what?' Lovell scrambled out of the hole, dejected. 'He can't just leave us here.'

'That's what I was trying to tell you,' Jhy cried. 'Dash saw him preparing to leave. So *I* saw him, too.'

The ship seemed to defy every law of aerodynamics as it rose into the air. Lovell was sure he could see Axim Gruff's face through the cockpit windshield, grinning in triumph as it spun around and made for the horizon. Its aft thrusters blazed as it finally disappeared from view.

'Why would he do that?' Did Gruff know the gold was gone? Did he have anything to do with its disappearance? And, if so, why bother to bring Lovell to the asteroid? The old captain scratched his chin, bemused.

'Er, Lovell?' Clarence was looking about him. Strange lights were appearing all around. Small points of colour quickly resolved themselves into physical shapes. Four armoured enforcement officers appeared on the asteroid's surface, their faces obscured by the reflective visors on their helmets. As three of them kept their pulse rifles trained on Lovell's astonished companions, the last lunged quickly towards the old freighter captain, slapping a restrainer between his shoulder blades. With a flash of light and a sharp whistle, Lovell fell unconscious against the armoured figure, his hat falling to the dusty ground. At a nod from their leader, they thumped at the small transport devices on their chests. Then they, and their captive, simply disappeared.

II
BANGED TO RIGHTS

Lovell's head hurt.

'Where the hell am I?' he groaned. He heard his own voice echoing back at him. At first, he couldn't be sure if he had his eyes open or not. Slowly, as they grew accustomed to the dark, he could make out features around him. He was in a small room, lying on some sort of hard ledge protruding from one of the walls. He could make out the shape of a door opposite him, the light spilling in from around it the only source of illumination. Aside from a bucket by his bunk, there was nothing else in the room. Lovell tried to sit up, but found his hands were fastened together behind his back. It took an enormous effort to swing his legs to the floor, an effort that set his head pounding again. 'I feel like I've overdone it on the Greel,' he moaned. The very mention of the word reminded him of Axim Gruff and his escape from the asteroid. It was clearly Gruff who had alerted the police to Lovell's presence. The smile as he took off had confirmed it. No doubt he had been handsomely rewarded for the tip off. 'Never trust a man with a taste for cheap beer,' Lovell rasped as he rubbed his temples. Just who were his kidnappers? And where were his friends?

Lovell staggered to his feet and shuffled to the door, swaying uncertainly in the darkness. 'Hey!' he called, 'Let me outta here!'

A small hatch slid open in the door, and Lovell found himself blinking into the glare of a light in the corridor outside.

'John D Lovell,' came a disembodied, mechanical voice. 'Detention chamber 14b.'

'Detention chamber?' Lovell leaned against the door, straining to see through the hatch. He could just make out other doors stretching away to his left and right.

'Trial, imminent,' concluded the voice, and the hatch snapped shut.

'Trial?' spluttered Lovell. 'What trial?' He slammed against the door with his shoulder. 'Let me outta here! I'm a goddamn hero!'

As if in response, the door slid open. Lovell reeled in the full glare of the lights, screwing his eyes up involuntarily. A humanoid robot stood, silhouetted in the doorway. As it moved over the threshold, Lovell saw it rolled on wheels and was dressed in a black tunic. A set of keys hung from a belt round his waist.

'John D Lovell,' it said. 'You are commanded to the courtroom.'

'What the hell's going on?' Lovell snarled. 'What have you done with my friends?'

'Trial, imminent,' the robot repeated.

Lovell was getting impatient. 'Whose trial?'

The robot raised its hand to point a gun at Lovell's chest. 'Yours.'

Lovell heard a beep from behind him, followed by a sharp electric shock to his wrists. He winced in pain.

'Come with me,' the robot commanded as the handcuffs sparked again. Lovell gasped. 'You only have to ask,' he hissed through gritted teeth.

The robot waved his gun and Lovell stepped into the corridor ahead of him. Stopping to lock Lovell's cell door behind him, the robot then spun round and jabbed Lovell in the back with his gun. 'Walk,' he commanded.

'Hey!' Lovell protested. 'Don't I get a lawyer? What about my one comms call?'

'Your advocate has been assigned,' the robot informed him.

'Oh,' Lovell sniffed. 'That makes me feel a whole lot better. Any chance of you telling me what I'm charged with?'

'Trial, imminent,' the robot replied.

'Yeah,' Lovell sighed. 'So you told me.'

They passed through corridor after corridor, each of them lit with harsh strip lighting embedded in the ceiling. Every now and then, Lovell heard banging and shouting from the many cell doors they passed. He wondered if his friends were behind any of them.

At last the maze of corridors led to a holding area where Lovell was handed over to another robot.

'I am the clerk of the court,' it announced. Aside from a black robe and ridiculous white wig, it looked the same design as Lovell's escort. 'I shall be keeping a record of your trial.'

'When do I choose my advocate?' Lovell asked as he was shuffled towards a large, metal door. He was certain he could hear the rising hum of conversation as he drew nearer.

'Your advocate has been assigned,' the clerk replied in the same metallic tones.

'Wow.' Lovell whistled through his teeth as he looked the two robots up and down. 'You guys are some double act.'

The door hissed open as Lovell spoke, forcing him back into the corridor as a fellow inmate was bundled out by two security robots. Lovell noticed they were exactly the same design as the two he had already met.

'I've been framed!' the young woman was yelling. 'That wasn't a trial!'

'Your sentence has been determined,' replied one of the robots in a cold monotone that Lovell recognised.

The woman twisted in her restraints until there was a sudden beep and a pulse of light. Her eyes rolling back into her head, the unfortunate prisoner arced her back as her handcuffs delivered a shock to her nervous system. Lovell thought she was going to collapse.

'That was no trial!' She cried in pain. 'I'm innocent!'

'Your sentence has been determined,' the robot repeated as it prodded her forward down the corridor. Lovell shuddered to think what that sentence might be. He also wondered what she had done. He had a bad feeling about the whole situation.

'Hey,' he stammered to the court clerk, 'if this is about that speeding ticket in the Delban Cluster, I'm sure we can come to an arrangement.' He leaned forward, lowering his voice to a confidential whisper. 'I'm on first name terms with the Kestran President.'

Ignoring him, the robotic clerk raised his hand to bang on the door. As it slid open, the hubbub from the expectant crowd rose in volume.

'I wasn't expecting an audience,' Lovell admitted as he was pushed towards a small booth in the centre of the room. As the conversation died away, he had the chance to look around. He found himself in a cavernous hall, dominated by a huge, stained-glass window. He had no idea if it was daylight that streamed through the coloured panes. With a shock, he realised he still had no idea where he was. From the architecture, he guessed it wasn't a space station. Was it Kestra? He glanced around the assembled crowd, but could see no evidence of the Kestrans' almond shaped eyes. They were an assortment of races dressed in a myriad of uniforms and casual clothes. Some pressed forward to the front of the crowd, others lifted their children onto their shoulders for a better view. It was clear they were here to enjoy the spectacle. Confused, Lovell looked behind him to see what the show was. Then he realised it was him. A creeping feeling of dread made his blood run cold. Looking to his right, he saw some familiar looking robots seated on a rostrum. Ridiculously, they were dressed in formal attire; buttoned up shirts, ties and tunics. Making a point of counting them, Lovell realised they were sat in two rows of six. Twelve jurors, he sighed to himself. Robotic court officials buzzed about the place, passing bits of paper and consulting in conspiratorial whispers.

The clerk of the court seemed to clear his throat. 'Members of the jury,' he intoned with some volume, 'lords, ladies and gentlemen, please stand for His Honour, Galactic Justice Tamar Beetrox!'

Lovell blinked. This seemed half way between a trial and an entertainment. A literal show trial. But, what was the charge? Lovell shifted guiltily on his feet as he realised it could be any number of things. He had not led an entirely blameless life.

To thunderous applause, two huge doors swung open towards the back of the hall, admitting great puffs of theatrical smoke designed to enhance the mood. The room was ablaze with coloured lights that pulsed in time to a ridiculously cheesy fanfare. Squinting through the haze, Lovell saw an oversized amphibian dressed in a long, red robe. Justice Beetrox stood for a moment in a spotlight, drinking in the adulation. His hands on his hips, he looked even wider than his round belly suggested. His eyes swivelled in their sockets as he stretched his mouth into a wide, toothy grin. Finally, he walked forward to take his place on an ornate throne, his wide frame barely contained by its plush, upholstered seat.

In a theatrical gesture, Beetrox lifted his gavel high into the air then, to yet more applause and whoops of excitement, brought it crashing down on the desk that stood before him. The Galactic Justice waited for the crowd to fall into an expectant hush, then leaned forward onto his fleshy elbows.

'The prisoner will state his name,' the great toad belched.

The old captain swallowed. 'Lovell,' he said. 'John D Lovell.'

The crowd erupted into a chorus of jeers and whistles. Beetrox silenced them with a knock of his gavel, then sat back in his throne to address the clerk of the court.

'And the charge?' he rumbled. Lovell could feel the spectators leaning forward in anticipation.

'Theft!' the clerk called into the expectant silence, and there was a collective groan of disappointment. They had clearly been hoping for something more salacious. 'And murder!' the clerk added, to huge cheers from the audience.

'Murder?' Lovell was incredulous. He had never knowingly murdered anyone. His mind raced guiltily back to his assault on the Zargon fortress. But, surely that was different. Wasn't it?

'And, who is the plaintiff?' Justice Beetrox licked his lips.

In response, the robot lifted a computer pad to read from the scrolling text. He sounded like he was introducing a contestant on a game show. 'All the way from Melvos Four, Ro Silvari!'

Lovell's eyes were wide in disbelief. That was a name he thought he would never hear again. Silvari was here? Once again, the great doors swung open at the back of the hall. Smoke flooded into the room as a tall, haughty looking woman with cropped hair walked towards her place in the court, waving at the spectators in their galleries.

Lovell looked closer. 'Ro!' he called. 'Am I pleased to see you?' He could see the woman was thinner and greyer than when they had last met, but she was still instantly recognisable. 'Hey, Ro, you've got to get me out of here!'

Ro Silvari folded her arms across her chest. It didn't look particularly like she was on Lovell's side.

'What is your complaint against this man?' Beetrox jabbed a warty finger at the defendant in the dock.

Silvari took a breath. This had clearly been a long time coming. 'He stole my ship,' she cried, 'and murdered my husband.'

There was a whoop of joy from the assembled crowd. This was evidently just what they wanted to hear. The cheers dissolved into hissing as the throng turned their attention back to the man in the dock. It seemed they had already tried him in their own minds and found him guilty.

Beetrox smacked his lips. 'How do you plead?'

Lovell was at a loss. 'Er, not guilty?'

There was much tutting from the audience.

'I *borrowed* her ship from her husband,' Lovell clarified. 'And Threep Silvari was a friend.'

'Oh,' Silvari scoffed. 'If you borrowed it, then I would like it back.'

Lovell thought of his beloved B156 Transporter smashed into the wall of the Zargon fortress. 'I had a bit of an accident,' he sighed. 'Come on, Ro,' he pleaded, 'there's no need for all this. Why don't we just sit down and talk, huh?'

'It's too late for that, Lovell,' Silvari snapped back.

Justice Beetrox banged his gavel for calm. 'Let the prosecution speak,' he grunted.

With a hum of servos, a robot whizzed softly to Silvari's side. Like the clerk of court, it wore a white wig on its head and a black gown was draped across its shoulders. Lovell thought the whole thing was getting ridiculous.

'My client,' the robot began, 'alleges that the defendant, Mr John D Lovell, did steal her Transporter. She maintains that the ship was, in fact, never her husband's to give away.'

Lovell blinked, sensing trouble.

'I would draw Your Honour's attention to Exhibit One in the inventory.'

As the robot spoke, an image of a legal document appeared on a screen behind Lovell for the whole court to see. Galactic Justice Beetrox leaned over his desk to swipe at a computer pad. Even from where he stood, Lovell could see he left a film of slime over the screen.

'Deeds of property,' Beetrox chuckled, 'for a B156 Transporter. Issued seven years ago in the name of Ro Silvari.' He nodded wisely as the crowd muttered among themselves. 'The evidence seems incontrovertible.'

'Wait,' Lovell interjected. 'Don't I get my say?'

Beetrox banged his gavel to quieten the jeers from the audience. 'Your advocate will speak for you in due course!' he roared.

'Furthermore,' Silvari's prosecution robot continued, 'we have video evidence of the defendant's part in Threep Silvari's murder.'

'That's impossible!' Lovell shouted. 'I played no part in Threep's murder.' At a nod from Beetrox, Lovell felt a sudden electrical charge from his handcuffs. He arched his back in pain.

'Let us see this evidence,' the Justice growled.

As the lights in the courtroom dimmed, a flickering film started to play on the screen. Lovell turned for a better view, only to see an image of himself. He looked much younger, no doubt the court was alleging this was at the same time he stole the Transporter. He was apparently skulking in the shadows of a dingy shopping arcade.

'Where is that?' Lovell demanded. 'I have no memory of this.'

'Silence in court!' Beetrox demanded with a bang of his gavel.

As the film played, Lovell saw himself hiding in the shade of an alcove. He was clearly waiting for someone. Shoppers passed by, some alone, others with members of their families, friends or robots. Lovell thought he saw the flash of metal in his younger self's hand. He was filled with dread as he watched Threep Silvari walk the length of the boulevard towards him. Threep looked just as Lovell remembered him; rotund and jovial. He walked with a distinctive waddling gait, waving in greeting to passers by. That was Threep all right, Lovell smiled to himself. Turning off the main thoroughfare, his portly friend was now just feet away from the man in the shadows. Lovell's smile dropped. The courthouse watched in silence.

The Lovell on the screen was waiting for his chance. As the crowd thinned and Threep passed by, there was a flurry of movement from the shadows. The younger Lovell leapt from the alcove and grabbed at his friend. There were audible gasps as the video footage showed Threep Silvari being bundled into the shadows, his arms flailing around him.

'No!' Lovell breathed. 'This never happened.' He swung round to appeal to Justice Beetrox. 'None of this happened.'

Beetrox, along with everyone else in the courthouse, had his eyes glued to the screen. Lovell turned back to see a slick of blood oozing across the ground from the alcove. Then, almost nonchalantly, the younger Lovell stepped from the shadows and sauntered on his way. The screen went blank as the lights snapped back on. The only sound in the hall was from Ro Silvari. Her gentle sobs filled the air.

'I'm sorry you had to see that, Ms Silvari,' Beetrox rumbled. 'But it is necessary that all the evidence be considered.'

Silvari nodded. 'I understand.'

'Evidence?' Lovell seethed. 'The tape's been tampered with.' The sound of boos rose from the crowd as they made their feelings felt. 'You've got to believe me. I heard of Threep's death, but I was on the other side of the galaxy when it happened.'

Beetrox banged his gavel for quiet and leaned forward over his desk. 'You can prove that, Mr Lovell?'

Lovell sighed. Of course he couldn't. Threep Silvari had died while Lovell was on a smuggling run for the Destran Clan. Naturally, no records had been kept. The clan had called it 'plausible deniability'.

'Very well,' Beetrox continued. 'We may now hear from the defence.'

Lovell breathed a sigh of relief as his advocate whizzed to his side. It was, of course, a robot just like all the others.

'M'lord Justice,' it began, haughtily, 'the full penalty of the law can hardly be sufficient for the heinous, callous, unmitigatedly evil crime perpetrated by the despicable rogue whom we now see cowering before us in the dock.' A great cheer rose from the crowd and Lovell was sure he saw one or two hats thrown into the air. 'I rest my case,' the robot concluded.

'Wait. WHAT?' Lovell was aghast. 'I thought you were meant to be the counsel for defence?'

The robot turned to him. 'I am,' it announced as it spun back to Justice Beetrox, 'but this crime is so heinous that this is, in fact, the best defence that can be offered.' With that, the robot advocate turned and whizzed back to his place in the court.

Lovell looked at Ro Silvari in despair. As she held a handkerchief to her face, Lovell was sure he saw her smile.

Beetrox called for quiet. 'It is clear to me,' he began, 'that the defendant is guilty as charged and all that remains is for the jury to find him so.'

'You can't do that!' Lovell shouted, incensed. 'That wasn't a trial.' He felt another sharp shock to his wrists. 'Stop doing that!' he groaned in pain.

The whole courthouse seemed to turn as one to the jury. The twelve robots, looking ridiculous in their shirts, ties and smart jackets, went through the motions of conferring with each other.

'Have you appointed a foreman?' The clerk of the court enquired.

'I am the foreman,' a robot replied as it unfolded itself to stand before the court.

'And what is your verdict on the first count, that of theft?'

'Guilty,' the juror robot announced. Lovell wasn't at all surprised.

'And what is your verdict on the second count, that of the murder of Threep Silvari?'

The air felt heavy with expectation. The whole courthouse seemed to lean in to hear the response. Lovell rolled his eyes.

'Guilty.'

The court erupted. Members of the audience whooped and cheered. They clapped each other on the back with delight and even, Lovell noticed, embraced each other in triumph. He noticed money changing hands. Behind him, the word *'guilty'* flashed repeatedly on the screen. Strands of gold metallic ribbon and even balloons fell from the ceiling. Ro Silvari, forgetting for a moment that she was supposed to be the victim, reached behind to shake the hands of several spectators, a broad grin on her face. The whole thing was a sham.

'John D Lovell,' said the Galactic Justice, grandly, 'you have been found guilty on both counts.' Another cheer. 'You will therefore be taken from here to be held until a date can be set for your execution.' He banged his gavel and motioned to the clerk of the court. 'Take him down!'

The roar was deafening.

'I've been framed!' Lovell yelled above the din. 'That wasn't a trial!' As he felt another stab of pain from his handcuffs, Lovell realised those were the exact same words he had heard from the young woman who he had seen dragged from the court earlier.

III

PREPARATIONS

Grand Leutna Shavan stood on the bridge of the Zargon marauder ship. It was a nimble craft and virtually undetectable. She knew it could fly all the way to Kestra itself without registering on even their most sensitive scanning arrays. But that wasn't what she was planning. Today, her captain had set a course to the Wasteland, a barren patch of space between the Kestran system and the Zargon home world. As she stood on the raised platform, her hands clutching at the railing in anticipation, she let her eyes gaze across the star field before her. She knew from her history books that her ancestors had once gazed up into the night sky, too. They imagined the stars were points of light pricked into the great blanket of space. Beyond, lay the domain of the gods, where light prevailed. The stars afforded them a glimpse of the afterlife every night. Shavan almost laughed at their naivety. Now, the Zargon Empire held dominion over several of those points of light. It was a matter of contention that their nearest neighbour, Kestra, remained beyond the Empire's reach. Kestra lay beyond the sun that it shared with the Zargon home world, but it may as well have been parsecs away.

Shavan had been promoted to her place after her brother's death in the previous attempt to subdue the Kestrans. Grand Leutna Gahn had been careless. Ensconced in his asteroid fortress, he had underestimated the capabilities of a small band of rag-tag insurgents. He had thought of them as nothing more than a nuisance. Shavan bit her lip. She had reviewed the security transmissions from the asteroid herself. The memory of seeing her brother die at the hands of a simple mystic was still fresh. If Sumara had survived the encounter, she would have made it a matter of honour to kill him herself. An eye for an eye. Gahn had been careless and paid the ultimate price as a result. The mission had failed and he had lost his life. Shavan would not make the same mistake. John Lovell had become something of a reluctant celebrity on Kestra. Her spies had reported back on his stilting appearances on vidcasts and speaking tours. Using a few well-placed informants, Shavan had made sure the old captain was detained and imprisoned on trumped-up charges by the most corruptible court in the galaxy. He had been disgraced and deposed. In other words, he was out of the way. Like a snake without its head, Shavan hoped the insurgents would lose their enthusiasm without a leader. In fact, she was counting on it.

The new Grand Leutna looked down from her platform to the command deck beneath. 'Bring her round, Captain Thule,' she barked.

She felt the deck shift subtly beneath her feet as the pilot pivoted the craft. As she watched at the window, she saw a small rogue moon come into view. The target.

Turning to a computer console embedded in the wall, Shavan punched at a series of buttons to activate a holographic display. The top slid away from a nearby table to reveal an array of projectors. There, in the empty space above it, hung a live feed of the moon outside. Shavan nodded to herself. It was the perfect target in the perfect position. She had deliberately chosen a time when it would be hidden from the Kestrans by their shared sun. The rogue moon, Zargon scientists had calculated, had an eccentric orbit within and beyond the system, appearing only once every twelve hundred centuries. She was sure it wouldn't be missed.

Shavan looked up as Leutna Jaht joined her on the platform.

'Everything is prepared, ma'am,' he announced with a sombre tone.

'You're sure?' Shavan purred.

Jaht gave a nervous smile. 'Your accelerated time scale has been a challenge,' he said, carefully, 'but the odds of success are greater than the odds of failure.'

Shavan nodded. She wasn't sure she liked the sound of that.

'The future of the home world hangs on the Doomsday Device.' The Grand Leutna leaned towards her minion. 'Don't let me down.'

Jaht swallowed and pulled a computer pad from his pocket. 'Commence the demonstration,' he ordered. There was a bustle of activity on the flight deck below as preparations were made.

Shavan turned back to the window to observe the fruits of Leutna Jaht's labours. Distant at first, another object had moved into view. As it came nearer, it was possible to make out its shape in detail. It was a huge, disc shaped craft with four projecting arms that curled beneath it like claws. It was the first time Shavan had seen it in action. She had to admit she was impressed. As it made its way slowly across the vista of stars towards the rogue moon, she could see the ominous device was almost a quarter its size.

From the corner of her eye, Shavan saw Jaht speak into his computer pad. 'Activate.'

She could tell he was nervous. The device was entirely automated which, she felt, left much room for error.

Turning to the hologram, Shavan watched as the craft uncurled its four metal claws. Leaning in, she could see the individual mechanisms flexing and contracting to produce the movement in each mechanical arm. As they unfolded, they revealed the barrel of a plasma cannon on the underside of the device. Keeping one eye on the projection, she watched as a countdown in the corner of the large window indicated the distance to the moon.

'Contact in thirty seconds,' Jaht announced.

By now, the strange claws were completely extended, giving the object the appearance of a gigantic space spider. Shavan smiled at the allusion.

'Fifteen seconds,' came Jaht's trembling voice. It pleased Shavan that he was so anxious. Service to the Zargon Empire was not to be taken lightly. Excellence was expected, failure was punished. She thought once again of her brother.

'Ten, nine, eight…'

Through the window, the Grand Leutna could see the Doomsday Device was about to make contact with the lunar surface. At the vital moment, the moon's spin sent it over the horizon. She turned to the hologram and watched as the device's claws met and then dug into the lunar surface in much the same way as a snoeg hook clings to a snoeg. Shavan shook her head at the childhood memory. There were no snoegs left on the home world now. In fact, there was very little left of anything. She peered closer to see the huge machine settling in the moon dust, anchored by the enormous pincers dug deep into the rock.

Leutna Jaht breathed a sigh of relief. 'Contact,' he snapped. In truth, he knew the real test was yet to come. He lifted his computer pad. 'Commence phase two.'

Even with the spin of the moon, the Grand Leutna could see the glow over the horizon. Untold amounts of energy were slamming into the rock, sending plumes of debris spinning off into space. Shavan looked back at the hologram spinning on the table. There, the progress of the device was much clearer. A devastating beam was drilling down into the lunar surface from its central cannon, obliterating everything that stood in its way. The rock became a seething mass of molten lava, only for that too to be boiled away. The plasma drill was carving its way through the moon like a knife through a Lanta egg.

'One hundred kilometres,' Jaht announced, a sheen of sweat on his upper lip. The gouge in the rock was as wide as a small continent and getting deeper with every second that passed. Shavan allowed herself, just for a moment, to be swayed by her better nature.

'You have done well, Leutna Jaht,' she soothed.

Leutna Jaht allowed himself a smile in response. 'Five hundred kilometres,' he reported.

Shavan looked on, enthralled, as the beam's progress was indicated through the heart of the holographic moon. Just as it reached the very centre of the moon, it stopped.

'We have now reached the core,' Jaht exclaimed as he checked his computer pad. He swiped at a button. 'Commence stage three.'

At his command, Shavan saw the nozzle that housed the plasma cannon split into four parts like the petals of a flower. Now an enormous grappler, it was lowered into the lunar core on lengths of cable that, in themselves, were many metres thick. The cables were unspooled at such a speed that they had dropped the grappler fifteen hundred kilometres in just a few minutes.

Shavan reached out to the holographic display with her fingers bunched. As she opened her palm wide, the image zoomed below the crust to the core. There, she could see the grappler grabbing at the material of the core; great shovels the size of small countries scooping at the partly molten rock and iron alloy. Then, the cables were spooling back into the huge disc above, bringing with them uncountable quantities of core material.

Shavan turned back to the window as the massive craft hauled itself from the lunar surface, its crab like pincers letting go of the surface rock as huge thrusters were activated around the rim. Behind it, as it lifted into black space, the moon lost its structural integrity. With a good portion of its core gone and a great welt carved from its surface to the centre, it collapsed in on itself. The crust gave way. Great boulders split from the rock to spin away into the void, leaving huge dust clouds in their wake. Soon, there was nothing left but a loose collection of rock and debris turning slowly where the moon had been.

The cause of its destruction, the huge Doomsday Device, was lifting clear of the dust, a huge chunk of the lunar core clutched in its mechanical claws.

'Report,' Shavan barked at her subordinate.

Leutna Jaht consulted his computer pad. 'Excavation is complete,' he sighed with relief, mopping the sweat from his lip with a sleeve. 'We have extracted two trillion tons of material from the moon's core.'

Shavan smiled. 'Excellent. And will the effect be as devastating on Kestra?'

Jaht swallowed. 'The moon was a quarter Kestra's size. There will be catastrophic damage to much of the planet. Over time, however, the tectonic forces around the well could split it in two.'

Grand Leutna Shavan nodded. Perhaps, at last, balance would be restored to the system and the Kestrans would get their just deserts.

'So, we are ready to move forward.' It was more a statement than a question.

'I would advise a final maintenance pass,' Jaht replied. 'But then, yes, all should be ready.'

A sudden alarm sounded from the flight deck. Jaht's computer pad flashed an ominous red.

'What is it?' Shavan looked at the holographic display in search of answers. She could see one of the grapplers was hanging loose, causing the payload to slip. The craft, suddenly unstable, lurched off course.

Jaht was leaning over the railing to the flight deck below. 'Let it go!' he yelled to the technicians.

'We've lost control,' came the response.

Jaht knew the technicians beneath him were merely relaying messages from the control room on the Zargon home world. It didn't make them any easier to bear. 'Tell them to try the backup program,' Jaht called, the panic rising in his voice.

'No response.'

Leaning towards the hologram, Shavan saw the grappler bending with the strain. Then, it snapped off entirely. As the mechanism spun away, the mass of semi molten rock was sent hurling towards the marauder.

'We've lost all guidance systems,' came the report from below.

Turning to the window, the Grand Leutna saw the huge device hanging, helpless, suddenly inert in space.

A computer voice rang out through the ship. 'Collision imminent! Collision imminent!'

The great ball of rock was heading straight towards them.

'Captain Thule, get us out of here!' Shavan yelled, gripping the railing. 'Now!' Leutna Jaht clicked his heels together in response and gave a smart nod of his head. 'And get that thing fixed!'

As Jaht left the platform, Grand Leutna Shavan turned back to the huge window. As the ship turned away from the disintegrated moon and the threat of the advancing core, she raised her wrist to speak into her personal comms.

'This is Shavan,' she hissed. 'I want to personally oversee the repairs to the device.'

'Yes ma'am,' came the response.

'Have Leutna Jaht detained upon our return.' She snapped off her comms, then thought again. Failure should be punished. She raised her wrist. 'In fact,' she snarled, 'kill him.'

IV
DOING TIME

The Saddle Nebula was billions of light years from anywhere. Situated in the far reaches of the galaxy, this inconsequential cloud of cosmic dust wasn't on anyone's list to visit. Surrounded by vast tracts of open space, it was renowned for being one of the quieter corners of the universe. Cold, remote and isolated, it was the perfect place to build a high security prison.

Hanging in the vast emptiness, the Nebula Penitentiary was a holding place for the dregs of the galaxy. The worst of the worst were held in cells just big enough for two, many of them waiting for their execution. It was a wheel shaped construction, with cells around the other rim. The inner hub was given over to exercise yards and open space, a vast dome looking out into the depths of space. To the inmates, it was known as The Neb. All were being held until their execution. All protested their innocence.

Prisoner 403 stood before Governor Dravit, a tall, gaunt looking man with fierce eyes. The Governor was dressed in an old-fashioned three piece suit. In fact, thought Prisoner 403 as he looked around him, the whole office was old-fashioned. Wood panelled walls had been fixed to the metal bulkheads and a carpet placed on the floor. An ornate chandelier hung from the ceiling, illuminating a series of vintage pictures that were fixed to the walls.

'John D Lovell,' Dravit wheezed through a cloud of cigar smoke. 'That is the last time you will hear that name.' He paused for a smile. 'Until your execution.' Lovell nodded. He had been ordered into a pair of grey, prison issue overalls. 'You are Prisoner 403.'

'What's in a name?' Lovell grinned. Beneath the bravado, he was despairing at the turn of events.

'You *have* no name,' Dravit continued, almost talking over him. 'You will be stripped of your personality and stripped of your rights. You are no one.'

Lovell shrugged. 'I know a lot of people who'd agree with you there.'

Dravit stood behind his large, wooden desk. Lovell noticed cigar ash on his lapel. 'There are no rewards here for good behaviour,' the Governor intoned. 'Good behaviour is expected. Bad behaviour is punished. Your first transgression will be rewarded with twenty-four hours in solitary confinement. Your second, forty-eight hours. Your third, four days and nights. And so it increases exponentially. By your sixth, you'll be in solitary for a month and your life won't be worth living. That is all you need to know.'

Lovell opened his mouth to talk.

'Of course, you're innocent,' Dravit interrupted him. 'Every man and woman in this prison is innocent, but there's something you should know.' He had walked right up to Lovell as he spoke and now they stood almost nose to nose. 'I don't care.'

Lovell resisted the urge to hit him. He'd met this type before; arrogant, self-assured, untouchable. Lovell wondered if he was part Zargon.

'Of course, in time, your thoughts will turn to escape.'

Lovell smiled to himself. His thoughts had already turned to escape.

Dravit sat back at his desk. 'A word of advice. Don't bother. No man has ever managed it.' He clicked a button on his desk, and a screen sprang to life behind him. It showed a picture of a swirling galaxy. 'You'll recognise this, of course,' Dravit coughed. 'This is Kestra, where I believe you've been spending a lot of time recently.' A small dot was glowing red towards the middle of the spiralling stars. 'This is the Neb.' The picture zoomed out, and kept zooming out. Soon, the galaxy was a small speck of light on the left hand side of the screen. Another small red dot glowed on the right hand side. It was labelled, *Nebula Penitentiary*. 'Sure, a modern ship could make the journey in pretty short time.' Dravit leaned forward on his elbows. 'But you have to remember this. No one knows you're here.'

Lovell was crestfallen. Dravit was right. From the moment he had been grabbed from the surface of the Zargon asteroid, he had been missing in action. His friends, presuming they had made it back to Kestra, would be none the wiser.

Dravit seemed delighted to see the colour draining from Lovell's face. 'Welcome to The Neb, 403.' The Governor waved his hand to indicate the induction was over.

Lovell grit his teeth, digging deep for his last vestiges of defiance. 'That's *Mister* 403 to you,' he snarled.

That single remark earned Lovell twenty-four hours in solitude. He was thrown into a dark cell with no windows and no heating. Pressing a hand to the outside wall, he could tell from the intense cold of the metal that there was nothing beyond but the vastness of space. His teeth chattered all night, even when he was in the midst of a fever dream. It featured tumbling towers of rock and huge expanses of empty space. Just as he began to think he had never felt so lonely, the stars seemed to coalesce into a face he recognised. Ro Silvari, her head thrown back in a long, triumphant laugh. Lovell woke with a start to find he had curled himself into a ball against the cold. He had no idea what time it was or how long he'd be left there. In fact, there was a lot he didn't know. Had his friends been taken captive, too? Why had Ro lied in court? And where was Lovell's gold?

'Hi, I'm Zoopy Lefrew.' The strange little man tapped the badge on his overalls. 'The guards know me as Prisoner 808.'

Lovell sat at the long table in the canteen, a bowl of uninspiring breakfast before him. 'Lovell,' he breathed, his bones still sore from a night on cold metal. '403.'

'I hear you've upset the Governor already.' Zoopy seemed impressed. 'Way to go. May I?' The little man nodded at the empty space next to the old captain.

'Sure.' Lovell scooted to one side.

'So, Lovell,' Zoopy began as he inspected his thin broth. 'What you in for?'

Lovell scratched his head. 'I'm not entirely sure.'

'Ha!' Zoopy's eyes lit up. 'Then you'll fit in perfectly.' He clapped Lovell on his shoulder. 'By the way, you want the good news or the bad news?'

Lovell took a spoonful of his food and winced at the taste. 'Er, the bad news, I guess.'

'You gotta share a cell.'

Lovell groaned as he looked around him. The room heaved with menace. There seemed to be hundreds of inmates all jostling for elbow room at the long canteen tables. Men and women of all sizes sat in their grey overalls, trying to raise enthusiasm for today's menu. The uneasy truce had already been broken once, when a fight had broken out in a corner between a man as big as a hovertruck and a woman covered in lurid tattoos. The great lump of a man had taken the woman by the throat and pushed her up against the wall. Lovell watched in horror as he had reached for the woman's hand and removed the spoon she had clutched there. They were fighting over the cutlery? As Lovell looked on, the guards had rushed them with their taser truncheons, jabbing at their ribs and shoulders in an effort to defuse the situation. In truth, it had only made things worse. The huge man had fallen onto his table, sending bowls of thin slop flying into the air. The other inmates, furious at the interruption to their meal, had joined the fray. It was only a matter of time before the Governor himself had appeared with a larger contingent of guards. In time, they had quelled the riot and bundled the monster of a man from the room. A barely controlled calm had descended once more.

'And the good news?' Lovell daren't think what was coming.

Zoopy nudged him with a bony elbow. 'I'm your cellmate!'

For the first time, Lovell looked his companion up and down. He had a lined but friendly face, framed with a frizz of wild, curly hair. He squinted up at him through a pair of thick spectacles. Lovell smiled. He could do worse, he guessed.

'So, you gonna show me the ropes?'

'Sure thing,' Zoopy beamed. 'You don't spend twenty years here without learning a thing or two.'

'Twenty years?' Lovell dropped his spoon, aghast. 'What did you do?'

Zoopy chuckled. 'Honestly? I can't remember.' He pointed to the guards posted around the room. 'And, luckily, neither can they. I should have been dead years ago. I guess I slipped through the cracks.' He leaned towards Lovell, his voice low. 'And I can teach you how to do it, too.'

Lovell sighed. He wasn't sure if he wanted to slip through the cracks if it meant spending decades in this hellhole. Mind you, the alternative wasn't that much better, either.

'I see people come,' Zoopy was continuing, 'and I see them go. Some are here a few years, others for just a few weeks. But it always ends the same way.' He looked suddenly sad. 'That's why I don't tend to make friends. I keep myself to myself as best I can.'

Lovell suddenly felt sorry for him. What must that do to a man? He lowered his voice. 'Have you never tried to, you know, get out?'

Zoopy gave an easy laugh. 'Why should I?' he asked in all innocence. 'I have no memory of life before The Neb. I'm fed and kept warm. I know my place. So long as I keep slipping through the cracks, I'm safe. But, out there…' he shivered as he pointed towards the door. 'Who knows?'

'Ain't no place to go, anyhow,' came a voice from the other side of the table. It belonged to a woman with high cheekbones and a tapered face. 'We're light years from nowhere with no means to get a message out. Didn't Dravit give you the talk?'

Lovell nodded, resigned. 'No one knows we're here.'

'We're off the grid,' the woman concluded. 'Outta sight, outta mind.'

'In other words,' chirped Zoopy Lefrew, 'you might as well get comfy. Your pack will have been delivered to our cell by now. I'll help you unpack after we've eaten.' He licked his lips as he gestured to Lovell's half full bowl. 'Speakin' of which…'

'Huh?' Lovell looked up to see the little man waiting eagerly. 'Oh, sure,' he said, pushing his bowl to Zoopy. 'Fill your boots. I seem to have lost my appetite.'

Just as Lovell's new cellmate was about to tuck in, something flew through the air to land in the food with a plop.

'Hey!' exclaimed Lovell as he looked up at the woman opposite. Seeing her peering over her own shoulder, he followed her gaze to a thickset man sitting on a parallel table. Alarmingly, one entire side of his face seemed to be made of metal.

'I know you,' the man snarled.

Zoopy took a breath. 'That's Gomo,' he whispered. 'He's part cyborg. Whatever you do, don't get on the wrong side of him.'

Lovell thought better of provoking an altercation. 'Don't think so,' he called back. The man was standing now, his hands planted on the table before him. Lovell couldn't help noticing they were the size of shovels. And one of them was entirely mechanical.

'Yeah, I know you. I spent some time on Kestra these last few months. You're a goddamn hero.'

Lovell felt all eyes upon him.

'A hero?' gasped Zoopy, clearly impressed.

'I wouldn't say that,' Lovell stammered.

'Yeah,' Gomo continued, much to Lovell's annoyance. 'I saw you on the vidcasts.' He was suddenly more threatening. 'You sure like to shoot your mouth off.'

Lovell spread his arms wide. 'Look, they wanted to ask me some questions, that's all.'

'A goddamn hero,' the man repeated, slowly clapping his hands together in mock applause. 'It's just a shame my cousin ain't alive to see it. The great John D Lovell, brought to The Neb.'

Lovell blinked. The guy knew his name. The old captain tapped his badge with his spoon. 'Prisoner 403,' he smiled, weakly.

'Er, Lovell,' said Zoopy beside him. Lovell looked down to see he had fished a metal badge from his soup. He recognised the insignia.

'Yeah,' the man called over. 'My cousin fought with the Zargon Empire. He hated those almond-eyed Kestrans almost as much as I do.'

Lovell swallowed. This wasn't going well. He flicked his eyes around the room, hoping the guards had noticed.

'That's his cap badge,' Gomo boomed, pointing at the insignia that Zoopy was turning over in his hands. 'He was a security officer. Worked hard, made his way up to Under-Leutna.' He leaned forward on the table. Even from this distance, Lovell could hear it creaking beneath his weight. 'He died in the battle for the Zargon asteroid.'

Lovell felt his heart in his mouth. Suddenly, he was running through those tunnels again, his friends beside him, the robot dog scooting ahead for signs of danger. Light grenades flashed in the air. Ice bullets fizzed past his ear to embed themselves in the rocky walls. All around him as the little team progressed through the asteroid stronghold, Zargon soldiers fell to the floor in their tens. No, in their hundreds.

'We... did what we had to do,' Lovell stuttered.

'Yeah?' Gomo bellowed. Finally, Lovell noticed he had drawn the guards' attention. 'Then, it looks like I'm gonna do what *I've* gotta do.' Gomo cracked his knuckles, menacingly. 'Not here, not now,' he sneered. 'But somewhere, and *soon*.'

With that, and with one eye on the advancing guards, Gomo sank to his seat. His cronies leaned into him, offering their support. They slapped him on the back and stared across the tables towards Lovell. He saw one of them, a skinny man with a scar across his face, drawing his finger across his throat in an implicit threat.

'Let's get outta here,' Lovell whispered to Zoopy. 'Breakfast is over.'

'A hero?' Zoopy Lefrew stood in his cell, seeing his cellmate in a whole new light.

Lovell dismissed the word with a wave of his hand. He lifted his pack onto the small table beneath the even smaller window. 'You said you were gonna show me the ropes?'

'Sheesh, I dunno,' chuckled Zoopy, scratching at the back of his neck. 'Seems like you could teach *me* a thing or two, hero.'

Lovell sighed. 'Look, this cell is barely big enough for the both of us. If we're gonna make it through in one piece, you're gonna have to drop the whole hero thing, okay? I just did what I had to.'

'I've heard of the Zargons,' Zoopy shrugged. 'They sound like the worst of the worst.'

'That's about right,' Lovell agreed as he zipped open his pack. 'What's all this?'

Zoopy swung himself up onto the top bunk. He was clearly enjoying having company. 'Everything they think you'll need. Pillow, towel, safety razor, shaving soap.' He leaned dangerously over the edge of his bed. 'Most prisoners never get beyond their first bar.'

'That's it?'

'What more d'you need?'

Lovell grunted and looked around the small room. The round cabin window looked out into the emptiness of space. This far from Galactic central, there were precious few stars. He blinked. Had he just seen a light moving slowly in the distance? He shook his head as he lost sight of it.

'Who's this?' Lovell let his hands wander over a sculpture of a woman's head that stood on a small table. She had full lips and hair of loose curls.

'Oh, that's Marion.' Zoopy rested his chin on the back of his hands. 'She's my wife.'

'It's beautiful, Zoopy,' Lovell enthused, impressed. '*She's* beautiful.'

'She is.' Zoopy's eyes shone so much, Lovell wondered if he was on the point of tears. 'Or was. I don't know.'

'You don't remember?'

Zoopy shook his head. 'Nope.'

'You ever hear from her?'

'Nope. No one never hears from nobody.'

Lovell frowned. 'What's she made of?'

'Shaving soap,' Zoopy replied with pride. 'The prisoners I share with don't usually get through a whole bar before, you know.'

Lovell winced at the thought. 'But, the guards? Dravit told me there were no rewards in The Neb.'

'Like I said,' Zoopy sighed as he settled back into his pillow. 'I keep slipping through the cracks.'

Lovell sat on his own bunk. If Zoopy had been allowed to build and keep a model of his wife's head, and Gomo had been allowed to keep his cousin's Zargon cap badge, there was clearly a game to be played. It was just a matter of trying to work out the rules. He lay back on his bunk, fingering the Zargon badge that Zoopy had passed him on their return from the canteen. There was something about his new cellmate that he found endearing. He was even pretty good company. Lovell put his hands behind his head. There were three options open to him. Spend the next two decades cooped up with Zoopy (not ideal), face an execution chamber (outta the question) or escape. He didn't much like the sound of the first two options, but he had no idea how to effect the third.

Just as he felt like he might slip into sleep, Lovell was startled by a long alarm that seemed to come from all around him. It made his teeth shake.

'Come on, Lovell,' said Zoopy Lefrew as he swung himself from his bunk. 'No rest for the wicked.'

'So,' said Lovell, resigned at last to his predicament, 'give me the dos and don'ts.'

The alarm had sounded for exercise. Hundreds of prisoners had been funnelled from their cells to the central yard at the hub of the wheel. Some had headed straight for the sports courts to shoot hoops or to the running track to complete a circuit. Others loitered on the steps or stood in groups to catch up with the gossip. Lovell noticed armed guards posted high up on watchtowers. Beyond them, the great glass dome looked out into space, a reminder of quite how far from civilisation they were.

'Keep your own counsel,' Zoopy replied, obligingly. 'Never offer an opinion. Never make eye contact unless you're spoken to.' He nodded towards the towers. 'That includes the guards.'

They sat on a flight of metal steps at one end of the yard, blinking into the huge arc lights that hung from the glass dome.

'Be prepared to trade if there's something you want, but never give away anything of value.' Zoopy took his spectacles from his nose and wiped them on his overalls. 'Cultivate two noses. One for your food and another for trouble. If you smell trouble, give it a wide berth. Mind you,' he chuckled, 'you should do the same with most of the food.'

Lovell stretched his legs out in front of him. There was something he had been burning to ask. 'Zoopy,' he began. 'What's the average stay?'

Zoopy slipped his glasses back on. 'Stay?'

'Yeah, you know.' Lovell took a breath. 'How long do most prisoners get before they're *taken away*?'

'Oh, I see.' Zoopy seemed suddenly distant. 'Mostly a few weeks. Some, days.'

'Days?' Lovell was aghast. 'And you've lasted twenty years?'

Zoopy shrugged. 'I learned something quick which you blew at lunch today.'

'What's that?'

'How to be invisible.' Zoopy flashed him a toothy grin. 'I bet even Governor Dravit wouldn't recognise me if I brought him his dinner. And he knows everything that goes on here.'

Lovell shook his head. 'I gotta get outta here, and quick.'

'Sure,' agreed Zoopy as if he'd heard it all before. To be fair, thought Lovell, he probably had. And many times over. 'But, how?'

'There's got to be a way.'

'Well, if there is, no one's found it yet. There are guards everywhere and cameras in every cell. There's a roll call every morning and night. Your bedding will be searched every day while you exercise. And let's say you do get out, what then?' Zoopy squinted up towards the dome. 'You'll be dead in an instant unless you get a suit. And if you get a suit, you'll be dead in days unless you got a ship. I doubt Dravit would even send the guards to get you. He'd assemble us all here and make us watch as you drifted away, into infinity.'

Lovell shuddered at the thought. 'I got friends,' he said suddenly. 'How would I get a message out?'

Zoopy considered the question as a game of blagball began on the court nearby. 'Bribe a comms officer, I guess.'

'With what?' Lovell asked, suddenly interested. If could get even a quick signal to Kestra, he could alert Clarence and Rudy.

'Well, that's the problem,' Zoopy was saying. 'What you got?'

Lovell was despondent. 'Nothing.'

'Nothing *yet*,' Zoopy corrected him. He looked around to check they weren't being overheard. 'Start small. Swap some bread for chocolate, swap the chocolate for soap. Soap buys tobacco, tobacco buys coin. Save enough, bribe the comms.'

Lovell swallowed. He may not have that long. 'There's money in here?'

Zoopy leaned closer. 'There's everything in here, Lovell. You just got to know where to look.'

As he gave an enigmatic wink, Zoopy felt a stinging blow to his cheek. Lovell looked up to see Gomo looming over them. He had retrieved the ball that had hit Zoopy and was now standing, menacingly, passing it from one powerful hand to another. At such close quarters, Lovell could see the tiny hydraulics extending and contracting as he flexed his mechanical fingers. Lifting his gaze still further, Lovell found himself staring into a lidless, cybernetic eye. One side of Gomo's face was a grisly metallic mask. The metal jaw adjusted its position as Gomo smiled.

'Hey,' he growled, 'hero.'

Lovell stood and dipped his head in something that he hoped looked like deference. In fact, it was fear. 'Hi,' he replied, bravely.

'You've gone and found yourself in the wrong place at the wrong time, Lovell,' Gomo hissed. His entourage had joined him now and they leered and cackled as their leader spoke.

'I'm just shooting the breeze with my friend,' Lovell insisted. He realised that they were leaving Zoopy completely alone, not even paying him so much as a glance. Looking down to his cellmate, Lovell saw that he was sitting stock still on the steps, his eyes cast down to the floor and his feet drawn in towards him. He was barely even breathing. Lovell understood at once. Zoopy Lefrew had made himself invisible. This was him, falling through the cracks.

'Better than shootin' Zargons,' Gomo rumbled. His cronies looked suddenly serious, their arms folded across their chests.

'Look,' Lovell began, 'I did what I had to do.'

Gomo had a far away look on his one organic eye. 'You know, it's always bothered me. I don't know how my cousin died. Was it in the fire fight, or was it in the explosions?'

Lovell gnawed at his lip. This wasn't going well at all.

'Perhaps you can help me out.' Gomo took a step forward. 'Perhaps you remember him.' He held out his mechanical hand at shoulder height. 'Little guy, but powerful. He had a scar on his eyebrow.' Gomo leaned in, his metal chin jutting forward. For the first time, Lovell got the impression that one of his legs was cybernetic, too. It would seem that the whole of Gomo's left side was robotic. 'Or did they all look the same to you?'

As Lovell searched for an answer, his thoughts were interrupted by the alarm. Exercise was over. Lovell breathed a sigh of relief and turned to leave the courts, only to find his way was obstructed by Gomo's outstretched arm. Lovell could only watch as the other prisoners made their way to their cells, Zoopy Lefrew among them. He gave an apologetic look over his shoulder, then fixed his eyes on the ground and shuffled to the exit. Lovell flicked his eyes to the watchtowers, only to see they had been abandoned. Indeed, every guard in the central hub had disappeared with the prisoners, leaving Gomo and Lovell alone by the steps. Lovell nodded in understanding. So, there was a game after all, and Gomo knew how to play it.

Before he knew it, Lovell took a blow to the stomach. Winded, he staggered forward, barrelling into Gomo with all his might. Maybe the guy's weight could be used to his advantage. Gomo stumbled backwards, the servos in his shoulder whirring as his arms flailed about him. Lovell ducked beneath them and ran for the games court. His eye had fallen on the one thing that might prove useful; a blagball racquet left behind in the rush to leave the exercise yard. It was three feet long and heavier at one end. Before he could reach it, however, Gomo was on him. He had dived for Lovell's legs and now had a hold of his left foot. The grip from Gomo's cyborg hand was intense. Lovell could feel his ankle being crushed. Gomo pulled the old captain towards him where he lay on the ground, a sickening grin on his face. Just as he reached out to grab him by the other foot, Lovell raised his shoe high in the air and kicked out at Gomo's cyborg eye. It shattered into tiny shards of glass and circuitry beneath his heel. In the shock, Gomo let Lovell go and scratched desperately at his face. He pulled the damaged eye from its socket and threw it to the ground where it sparked and fizzed in the dirt.

'I can always get another eye,' he rasped, mockingly as he advanced on Lovell. Lovell threw himself on the racquet. Clutching it in both hands, he swung for Gomo, leaning into the swing with all his weight. It made contact with Gomo's thigh with an audible *clang*. Where Lovell had hoped to meet muscle, he had met metal. Cursing, Lovell saw the racquet had bent out of shape. He swung wildly again as Gomo advanced, this time concentrating on the right hand side of his body. The human side. Gomo swept his cyborg arm before him to deflect the blows. Finally, he grabbed a hold of the racquet mid-swing and met Lovell's eye.

'Still a hero?' he leered.

Lovell took a breath. 'Nope. Just a guy trying to stay alive.'

With that, he let the racquet go. Gomo stumbled forward as Lovell ducked behind him. Taking advantage of Gomo's forward momentum, he raised his foot again to push him in the small of his back. The squat cyborg pitched towards the floor, but managed to turn himself face up as he fell. As Lovell lunged towards him, he found himself in Gomo's grip. His hands squeezed at Lovell's neck. Gomo shifted his weight, turning until he was on top of Lovell. The old captain felt his eyes bulging as Gomo's cyborg fingers squeezed tighter at his neck. Lovell felt the blood vessels in his face bursting with the pressure. His vision was fading. He clawed at the ground in desperation, then raked his nails across Gomo's face. He seemed completely unaffected. Lovell wished he had Rudy by his side. The demolition robot's brute force was the only thing that could save him now.

'This,' Gomo spat as he squeezed hard at Lovell's throat, 'is for my cousin.'

At such close quarters, Lovell could see right into the man's skull through his empty eye socket. The mention of Gomo's cousin seemed to sharpen Lovell's wits. As his head swam, he struggled to focus on a thought. Through the haze, he remembered the Zargon cap badge that Gomo had thrown at him that morning. In his mind's eye, he saw his cellmate twisting it in his hand, the metal glinting in the light. In what felt like his final breath, he remembered Zoopy passing him the badge in their cell. Lovell must still have it in his pocket. The realisation gave him a little strength. Perhaps there was life in the old dog yet. Fumbling for the pocket in his overalls, Lovell felt the smooth metal of the cap badge. His fingers were numb, but not so numb that he couldn't release the pin on the back. He only hoped it would be long enough to do some damage.

'He died for nothing,' Gomo was saying, oblivious to Lovell's plans.

'No,' Lovell rasped. 'He died trying to invade a sovereign planet.'

Gomo gave a dry laugh. 'You never ask yourself why?'

Lovell was perplexed.

'You never ask why they were invading?'

Lovell felt himself devoured by darkness. He had to strike now, but did he have the strength? Gomo thrust his face closer. 'Then I guess you'll never know.'

Lovell saw his chance. With Gomo's face so close, it was now or never. In a single, deft movement, Lovell drew the badge from his pocket, angled the pin away from him and plunged it deep into Gomo's empty eye socket. He felt the metal connect and there was a sudden spark from inside Gomo's skull. Lovell had gambled that Gomo's cyborg command circuits would be patched into his brain and that, with his eye gone, they would be exposed. Luckily, he had been proven right. A look of panic flashed across Gomo's face, his human eye blinking in confusion. A bolt of electric energy seemed to fizz down the man's entire left side. Lovell felt the grip on his throat loosen. With a roar, Gomo tilted to one side, leaving Lovell to scramble to his feet. Rubbing at his throat, he watched as Gomo lay on his back before him. The cyborg side of his body was completely inert, its sheer metallic weight pinning him to the ground. He kicked and scratched with his human arm and leg, but couldn't right himself. Lovell was reminded of a beetle on its back. Gomo gave a cry of desperation.

'Sorry to put a spanner in the works,' Lovell panted, his lungs burning. 'But it's what I'm good at.' With that, he turned towards the exit, trying his best to hide just how badly he was hurt. The gate swung open as he approached and Lovell saw a guard waiting to escort him to the Governor's office. This was Lovell's second offence. He knew he had just earned himself two days in solitary.

'You look awful.' Zoopy Lefrew peered up through the broken glass in his spectacles.

'I feel worse,' Lovell sighed. 'What happened to your glasses?'

'What can I say?' Zoopy shrugged. 'Casualty of war.' Lovell remembered them falling from Zoopy's face in the exercise court. 'But not as much as you.'

Lovell rubbed his neck as he limped to the bunk. A night on a cold, metal floor hadn't helped. He felt cold to the bone.

'Gomo got nothing,' Zoopy shrugged, 'except a few hours in the hospital workshop.' He chuckled. 'You damaged him good.' Zoopy reached into his pocket and drew out a chunk of bread. 'Hungry?'

Lovell grabbed it, gratefully. He had never felt his age quite so much.

'You've missed dinner,' Zoopy explained as he smoothed a nick in his sculpture. 'It's lights out soon.' The soft soap yielded to his touch as he gently reshaped his beloved's eyebrow.

'Suits me,' Lovell grumbled. 'I need some sleep.'

Zoopy looked at his cellmate with a smile. 'Here,' he said as he helped swing Lovell's legs onto his bunk. As the old captain drifted into an uneasy sleep, he caught a sight of the emptiness outside the window. There was that light again, moving faster now. And it seemed to be coming closer.

Lovell woke in a sweat, his heart pounding. He propped himself up onto his elbows, squinting into the gloom. From above him, came the sound of Zoopy snoring. As Lovell's eyes grew accustomed to the dark, he was sure he saw movement at the tiny window. He pushed back his covers and staggered to his feet, his head throbbing from the effort. Leaning against the window, he pressed his forehead against the glass. Yawning, he rubbed his eyes, only to find himself gazing into a familiar, robotic face. Beyond the glass, he saw a pair of mechanical eyes, flashing with excitement. The little robot's tail wagged giddily as it recognised Lovell. He could almost hear it yapping in the vacuum of space. Dash. Lovell gasped as the little dog disappeared from view. If Dash was here, that could only mean one thing. He turned as he heard the sound of the hatch on the cell door snapping open and shut. Someone was trying to get his attention.

'Hey!' called Zoopy groggily from his bunk. 'What's going on?'

Lovell frowned. He still wasn't entirely sure himself. 'We got guests,' he replied, carefully. He shuffled to the door as the hatch stopped rattling. Finally, it snapped fully open and a hairy hand reached through, clutching a piece of paper. It let go of the note and withdrew back through the letterbox, the flap clattering shut behind it. Lovell could barely contain himself. Bending to the floor, he picked up the piece of paper and called to his friend. 'Hey, Zoopy. Give me a little light over here.'

Zoopy flicked on his torch and angled it down from his bunk. Lovell held the paper up to the light to read the message. '*STAND BACK*,' it said, in a spidery scrawl that he recognised.

'What does it say?'

Lovell held up a hand to stop Zoopy climbing down. 'I'd stay right there if I were you,' he cautioned. Screwing up the piece of paper, Lovell made his way back to the window. He had no idea what to expect, but he guessed it was going to come through the door. How wrong he was. Pressing himself against the wall, he was confused by a sudden *clang* from the floor. It came again and again. Soon, the deck plate was buckling from the application of a massive force from beneath. A final blow tore the floor apart and a great metal fist emerged through the hole. Another hand joined the first in tearing the deck plates apart. In a matter of moments, the hole was large enough to admit a giant, marauding robot. Rudy hauled himself into the cell.

Lovell was aghast. 'Rudy!' he exclaimed. 'What the hell are you doing here?'

Rudy swung his great head round to face him. 'Sorry to interrupt,' he rumbled, 'but we are here to rescue you. Sir.'

Lovell punched the air. 'I knew it! I knew you'd come and get me!'

'We must go,' Rudy growled, his visual receptors blazing in the dark.

'Is that yours?'

Lovell turned to see Zoopy had jumped from his bunk. 'This is Rudy. He's a friend of mine.' He turned to lay his hand on one of the robot's huge mechanical arms. 'A good friend.'

'Is he taking you away?'

Rudy had already lowered himself back through the hole. 'We must hurry, sir,' he cautioned.

Lovell turned to his cellmate. 'Come with me, Zoopy. Get the hell outta this place.'

Zoopy sat on the bunk, downcast. 'But it's all I know,' he almost whispered. 'I've forgotten what life is like on the outside.' A sigh shuddered through his body. 'And I'm scared.'

'Of what?' Lovell reached towards him, imploring him to follow.

'Of remembering what I did.' Zoopy's eyes flicked to the soap sculpture. 'Lovell,' he stammered, 'I have a terrible feeling that I killed my wife.' Lovell saw tears welling in the little man's eyes. 'I'm worried that, if I get out, I'll remember what I did.' He wiped his damaged spectacles on a blanket. 'And I don't think I could live with myself.'

Lovell nodded, sadly. 'Okay, my friend,' he breathed. 'Then I wish you well.'

Zoopy swallowed back the tears. 'Go,' he said, at last, 'and forget all about this place.'

Lovell laid a hand on his cellmate's shoulder. 'I will try. But I'll never forget you.'

'Sir,' came Rudy's voice from the hole in the floor, beckoning him with a metal finger.

With a final look around the cell, Lovell followed his mechanical friend through the tear in the deck plates. Behind him, Zoopy gazed in awe as he made his escape. 'You'll always be a hero to me,' he muttered to himself.

'Where are we going?' Lovell struggled to keep up with the lumbering robot ahead of him.

'To the ship,' Rudy boomed. 'To freedom.' He led Lovell through a labyrinth of ventilation ducts that ran beneath the complex. Lovell had to crouch low to make his way through the shafts, his back aching in his unnatural posture. He noticed Rudy had almost folded in on himself, pulling his arms and legs tight into his body. Even so, he barely fit in the confined spaces and, once or twice, even banged his head on the lower portions of the metal duct. Eventually, they emerged into a maintenance hub. Great pipes hung from the wall, feeding into vast conditioning units. Lovell guessed they were in the ventilation control room.

'Hey, Lovell,' came a voice he had once feared he would never hear again. 'Fancy meeting you here.'

Lovell turned to see Clarence B Bond lowering himself into the room from a vertical shaft, a breather strapped to his hairy face.

'Clarence! Boy, am I happy to see you!' Lovell clasped the chimp to his chest. 'How did you find me?'

'You have the boy, Jhy, to thank for that,' Clarence smiled. 'Him and his robot dog.'

'What about the guards and the other prisoners?' Lovell cocked his ear to the ventilation shaft. 'Why's it so damned quiet?'

Clarence ripped his breather from his face and nodded to a corner of the maintenance hub. There, Lovell saw a gas cylinder lashed to the ventilation system. 'Halothane,' Clarence explained. 'It's an anaesthetic gas. We pumped it everywhere but your cell. The whole station is out like a light.'

Lovell was impressed. 'I guess Dash told you which cell I was in?' He remembered the dog's face peering in at the cell window.

Clarence nodded. 'We're quite a team, huh?'

Lovell looked at his friends. 'You sure are.' He looked around him. 'But how are we getting out?'

Rudy stamped a heavy foot. A flap rose from the floor in response. 'Refuse chute,' he boomed.

Lovell wrinkled his nose in disgust. 'Great.'

Rudy swivelled to face his master. 'After you, sir,' he said, reaching out to Lovell with his gargantuan hands. Ignoring the old captain's protestations, he lifted him clear off the floor then dropped him down the refuse chute. Lovell let out a cry as he fell, his elbows and knees chafing against the narrow tube. Even in his panic, he still found the time to wonder where he was headed. He was certain that The Neb, in common with all large space structures, would dump its rubbish straight into space. If this was the refuse chute, then he was bound for the coldness of the void. Lifting his hands to his face, Lovell screwed up his eyes in anticipation of the vacuum. Surely there was a plan?

With an unceremonious plop, John D Lovell found himself flailing on the floor in a small cargo hold. Springing to his feet in readiness for a confrontation, he found he was alone. He looked around at the gleaming white walls, panels of instrumentation blinking merrily. Wherever he was, it looked new.

'Pretty neat, huh?'

Lovell whirled around to see Clarence descending sedately from the ceiling. 'You've got ropes?' Lovell's jaw hung open. 'Why didn't you tell me you had ropes?'

'You didn't ask.' The chimpanzee gave a tug on the rope to pull it free and coiled it up in his long arms. Lovell was agog to see that, in comparison to his own dirty overalls, Clarence's white tunic had barely a mark on it.

'I'd stand back if I were you.' The chimp pulled Lovell gently back to a safe corner and waited. Rudy joined them with a *crump* that set the deck plates shaking. So, he was on a ship.

'Lovell!' The voice came from the hatch to the bridge. 'We found you! I knew we would!'

An overexcited Jhy ran into the cargo hold, throwing himself at Lovell's legs. His robot dog careened after him, his mini thrusters lifting him into the air so he could nuzzle at Lovell's face.

'Er,' Lovell spluttered, 'the family reunion is lovely, but shouldn't we be getting out of here?'

'There's no hurry,' came another voice he recognised.

Waving Dash away, Lovell turned to the hatch to see a tall woman with distinctive, almond-shaped eyes.

'Zana! What the hell are you doing here?'

The Kestran colonel moved to embrace him. She was in civilian clothes but still, Lovell noticed, she walked like a soldier. 'Well, firstly, I have to give you this.' She drew a hand from behind her back to present Lovell with his battered hat. 'Sorry about the dirt,' she said as he wiped the brim with a smile. 'Let's call it asteroid chic.'

'I'm glad you kept it,' Lovell said with a sincere smile. He jammed the hat on his head and adjusted it to what he considered to be a rakish angle.

'How could I not?' Zana leaned forward to kiss him on the cheek. Was it Lovell's imagination, or was there more to that kiss than friendly concern?

'And secondly,' Zana concluded as she beckoned him to the bridge, 'I've come to take you home.'

V
PLAYING WITH FIRE

'Leutna Jaht has been disposed of.' Under-Leutna Mev chose his words with care.

'Excellent,' Shavan snarled. 'Disseminate the news of his death far and wide.' She smiled as Mev snapped his heels together. 'You have finished the repairs to the device?'

Back on the Zargon home world, Grand Leutna Shavan had taken personal control of the project. It was, she had realised, the only way to get things done.

'Yes, ma'am,' Mev replied. 'A second test has been carried out. A comet in the Sturg Cloud.'

'Was it successful?' Shavan leaned over her desk, daring him on.

'Completely.' There was a note of relief in Mev's voice. 'I have sent the data for you to review at your leisure.'

Shavan stabbed at some controls on her desk. A three dimensional image appeared in the centre of the room. The Grand Leutna watched as the recording played. This time, all went to plan. The spider-like device latched on to the comet with its claws and drilled deep into the rock with its powerful plasma cannon. This time, the grappler retrieved the comet's core without a hitch and released it in a more controlled manner. As Under-Leutna Mev had stated, the operation had been a complete success.

'This pleases me,' Shavan breathed as she switched the recording off. 'You are to be congratulated on your success.' Mev clicked his heels again. Shavan was beginning to find it annoying. 'Can the device be concealed until the time is right? We cannot risk discovery.'

'Indeed, Grand Leutna,' Mev explained. 'Our technicians have been working on the creation of a gravity well. Once inside, the Doomsday Device will be safe from detection. Light itself will be bent around it, confounding any Kestran scanning device.'

Grand Leutna Shavan nodded. 'Impressive.' She turned to look out the window of her operations room. It looked out over one of the busier parts of Zargon City, the capital of the home world. Through the smog, she could see groups of guards standing on each corner. With the pollution and erratic energy supplies, people had been taking to the streets to protest. Such actions were forbidden, of course, and Shavan had personally given the order to fire upon the crowds more than once. Hundreds of citizens were arrested every day. Those that were found to have undermined the Zargon Elite were sent away, never to return. For the most part, the population was compliant but Shavan knew it wouldn't last. The Zargon Elite had squandered many of the home world's natural resources to build its fleet, only to have it destroyed just as it was ready to strike. John Lovell had a lot to answer for. A blanket of toxic gasses now covered the planet. Temperatures rose as the air became thick with pollutants. People died as a result and the hospitals were full of the sick. Shavan gnawed her lip. She knew the Empire's time was running out. As she saw it, she had just one more throw of the dice, maybe two.

Gazing through the window, the Grand Leutna suddenly saw Mev's reflection in the glass. Surprised that he was still in the room, Shavan spun round on her heels to face him. 'There is something else?'

Under-Leutna Mev cleared his throat and looked at the floor as he spoke. It was a gesture that worried Shavan no end,

'Grand Leutna,' Mev began. 'I must impart some unfortunate information.'

Shavan's eyes bore into him. 'Go on,' she dared him.

'There has been a defection from our science corps.'

Shavan shook her head in disappointment. 'Who is he?' she demanded.

'Not he, ma'am,' Mev said, carefully. 'They.'

Shavan felt the rage rising within her. 'How many?' she spat.

'Four, ma'am,' Mev stuttered. 'They served under Leutna Jaht.' He shifted uncomfortably where he stood. 'They were apparently unhappy with his treatment.'

'Unhappy?' Shavan shrieked, her face red with fury. 'It's not my place to keep people happy.' Sweeping a loose strand of hair from her face, the Grand Leutna attempted to regain her composure. 'Were they assigned to the Doomsday Device?'

'Yes ma'am.'

'Then I trust you have checked their work?'

'I have. It is sound. The device is safe.' Under-Leutna Mev felt suddenly vulnerable.

'Where have they gone?'

Mev swallowed. 'We believe they have fled to Yoba, a neutral planet beyond our system. The danger is that they may defect to Kestra and tell the enemy all they know.'

Shavan turned back to the window as she thought. 'Under-Leutna Mev, I want you to take personal responsibility for their capture and disposal.' She turned back into the room. 'Take as many soldiers as you need to infiltrate the Yoban system. Do whatever it takes to neutralise them. They must not make contact with the enemy.' She clenched her fist so hard that her nails dug into the palm of her hand. 'We have just days until Kestra is in the optimal position for us to strike. I will not see us fail again.'

'No ma'am.' Mev waited for the order to leave.

'Do you have family, Under-Leutna Mev?' Shavan sounded pensive.

'I have a wife and daughter.' Mev's voice caught in his throat. 'She is sick.'

'The pollution?'

Mev was suspicious of the Grand Leutna's caring tone. 'She was born with weak lungs. The quality of the air does not help.'

Shavan nodded as if she understood. 'Find those scientists and you will join the Elite. You and your family will be housed in a more *appropriate* residence. Air filters, security, an independent power source.'

'Thank you ma'am,' Mev stuttered in gratitude.

'But if you fail…'

The Under-Leutna was taken aback. It was as if a mask had slipped. Shavan's pretence at civility had fallen away. 'If you fail,' she snarled, 'your daughter will die. And you will have to tell your wife why.'

Mev was about to click his heels together again but a look from the Grand Leutna made him think twice. Instead, he settled for a curt nod of his head. The soles of his boots squeaked on the polished floor as he walked from the room, the sound of his heart pounding in his ears. The moment the door hissed closed behind him, Under-Leutna Mev leaned against the wall. He swallowed hard as his gorge rose in his throat. Settling his breathing, he straightened his tunic and wiped the sweat from his upper lip.

'Brunt?' he barked into a nearby comms panel. 'Assemble a squad and meet me in the briefing room in one hour. I've got a mission for you.'

VI
HOME SWEET HOME

Lovell lay back on the medbed, his wounds being tended to by a remarkably gentle Rudy.

'Hey, Rudy,' he smiled. 'You got a great bedside manner.'

'I have a good teacher,' Rudy muttered. If a robot could sound wistful, then that's exactly how Rudy sounded.

'You mean *had*,' Lovell corrected him, gently. He had fond memories of Sumara teaching Rudy to control his strength before he died on the Zargon asteroid. He taught him to pick up and let go feathers in an effort to teach him the subtle art of finesse. It had clearly paid off. One slip of his hand and Rudy could make Lovell's wounds worse. As it was, the giant robot was cleaning his grazes with a studied gentleness.

'No,' Rudy rumbled. 'Sumara is still with me. He is still my teacher.'

How about that? mused Lovell. *Whoever would have thought a robot could be sentimental?* He decided to let the matter go. Instead, he looked around the medbay. Like everything else on this strange craft, it was state of the art. The latest medical equipment stood ready for use, although it had clearly yet to be used.

'What is this ship?' Lovell asked no one in particular.

'Kestra's finest,' came the response. Colonel Zana had been watching from the door. 'Sanctioned by the President himself.' She sat on the edge of Lovell's bed and watched as Rudy cleaned his wounds. 'It's how we got to the penitentiary so quickly. Any other ship would have taken weeks.'

'Well, tell the President thanks from me.'

'You can tell him yourself,' Zana smiled. 'He's asked to see us.'

'Us?' Lovell scratched at the stubble on his chin.

Zana nodded. 'We're a team, remember?'

Lovell had to concede that she was right. And what a team they had been. But wasn't that in the past now? 'What does he want with us?'

Zana seemed to hesitate. 'There's trouble, John,' she admitted. The use of his first name perturbed him. 'It seems the Zargons aren't finished with Kestra.'

'Ah now, come on.' Lovell propped himself up on his elbows. 'Haven't I done my bit?' And paid for too, he thought, his mind flashing back to the vengeful Gomo in The Neb.

'Just hear him out, that's all I ask.' Zana flashed her almond eyes.

'Okay,' Lovell sighed. 'Now tell me one thing. How the hell did you find me?'

Zana laughed. 'Teamwork, of course.'

Lovell frowned, confused.

'It was Jhy who had the first breakthrough.' Zana made herself comfortable next to Lovell as she continued. 'We had no idea who took you from that asteroid, until Jhy realised that Dash had seen it all, too. He was able to view a replay of the events using his psychic link to the dog. He watched it again, sure that there was some sort of clue to be found.' Lovell was enthralled. 'Then he found it. The insignia on the guards' uniforms. He was able to draw it in detail. Clarence ran it through the Kestran mainframe and found it was attached to the Justice Collective.'

'The what, now?' Lovell was none the wiser.

'A mercenary police force for hire,' Zana explained. 'They're a feed for the Galactic Court. Once we knew that, Rudy was able to scan for the court broadcasts.'

Rudy looked up at the mention of his name.

'Wait.' Lovell was agog. 'You watched my trial?'

The Colonel nodded. 'If you can call it that. Oh, and I'm looking forward to hearing all about Ro Silvari.' She winked at Lovell, playfully.

'Don't remind me,' the old freighter captain sighed.

'Once we heard the verdict, we knew where you would be sent.'

'How?' Lovell asked. 'The Governor said once at The Neb, you'd never be found.'

'We got lucky,' Zana admitted. 'We knew someone who had been through the exact same process before. Trumped up charge, imprisoned at The Nebula Penitentiary.'

'But that's impossible,' Lovell scoffed. 'He'd be dead.'

'Unless he'd escaped.'

Lovell looked up to see Clarence B Bond leaning in the doorway. His eyes grew wide as the penny dropped. 'You were at The Neb?'

Clarence nodded. 'Long before we met. Murder charge. I was there for eighteen days which, if you ask me, was eighteen days too long.'

'But that's impossible,' Lovell cried. 'Governor Dravit said no man had ever escaped.'

'Oh, yeah?' Clarence laughed. 'Did you ask him how many chimps?'

Lovell nodded, suddenly understanding. He had a newfound respect for his simian friend.

'So, Clarence knew exactly where you would be being held,' Zana continued, 'and he knew you wouldn't be there long.'

Lovell remembered Zoopy Lefrew and how many fellow prisoners he had seen come and go. He shuddered when he thought how close he had come to being just another inmate, passing through The Neb on his way to an appointment with death.

'I petitioned the President to let me use The Valiant and, well, here we are.'

Lovell looked around him. 'This is The Valiant?'

Zana nodded. 'Beats an old B156 Transporter, don't you think?'

'I guess I could get used to it,' Lovell smiled back.

Zana got to her feet. As Rudy finished tending to his patient, the Colonel leaned over and smoothed Lovell's sheets around his shoulders. 'Get some rest,' she soothed. 'There's some fresh clothes for you in that locker. Get changed when you've slept, then come and join us on the bridge.'

The Valiant swooped gracefully between the gleaming mountains of Estoran, Kestra's capital city. To Lovell, it was a sight for sore eyes. There had been times in the last few days when he had wondered if he'd ever see the place again. Peering at the forward screen in the prestige cockpit, he was able to make out all the familiar landmarks; the monorail winding its way along the valley, the presidential compound nestling against the high slopes. As they drew nearer, he was able to make out the water parks and recreation grounds where the local population spent much of their leisure time.

Once the ship had landed on the pad, Lovell was amused to see the President's personal guard stationed either side of the boarding ramp. As he stepped from the craft, he was able to look back for his first external view of The Valiant. She was all gleaming metal and sleek lines, a pair of wings swept back into a delta formation. Her hull was coated in a reflective paint that Lovell had no doubt was instrumental in her capacity to avoid detection. Two powerful ion engines protruded from her aft section.

'She'll cover three parsecs before you've bent down to pick up your hat.' Clarence looked back with him. 'She's one of a kind.'

'I've got ship envy,' Lovell joked as he turned to join Zana, Rudy, Jhy and the chimp on the presidential shuttle. He noticed the pilot throw him a familiar look as he boarded. It was a look of respect that Lovell was not entirely comfortable with. He had seen it so many times since the destruction of the asteroid and the Zargon fleet. No matter how proud he was to have played a part in the operation, he felt distinctly unworthy of the adulation it had brought him. Clarence, on the other hand, seemed to lap it up. He'd even had a special pen made to sign autographs.

'As a military philosopher,' the chimp had told Lovell recently, 'I'm intrigued to find myself the subject of my own thesis.'

Lovell had grunted in response.

As the shuttle lifted off towards the presidential palace, Jhy came to sit next to the old captain.

'Colonel Zana tells me I have a lot to be grateful to you for,' Lovell grinned as he put his arm around the boy's shoulder.

Jhy looked thoughtful. 'I don't like gratitude,' he said at last. 'It kind of means that you're in my debt. We're equals.'

Lovell frowned. Just when had the kid got so wise?

'Besides,' Jhy continued. 'I am sure you would have done the same for me.'

'Yeah,' Clarence chimed in. 'Or me.'

'Or me,' added Rudy with his great bass voice.

Lovell nodded. Just six months ago, he wouldn't have been so sure, but now? Yeah, they were right. He would've done the same for any of them.

'Two minutes to landing,' the pilot reported from the cockpit. As the automatic landing procedures kicked in, he turned to Lovell and lowered his voice. 'Before you leave sir, would you mind recording a message for my wife? She's a big fan.'

The Kestran President, Lovell noticed, was dressed in casual clothes. Lovell had learned that everything had a meaning. Even the most trivial detail could speak volumes. Perhaps the President's appearance meant that this meeting wasn't entirely on the record. His jet black hair was swept back from a widow's peak. His presidential robes had been replaced by a simple white gown trimmed with gold, fastened at the waist by a wide leather belt.

'It is good to see you, Lovell,' he smiled as he extended a hand of greeting.

'Thanks for the welcoming committee,' Lovell replied, gesturing to the guards who had accompanied them from the shuttle.

'They're purely for your own security,' the President explained. 'You must remember, Lovell, you're something of a celebrity here. And now, you're a wanted man too.'

He led the little party into his private rooms where the lighting gave a soft glow to the walls. A collection of colourful rocks ringed a central water feature, studded with exotic plants and vibrant flowers. Jhy ran straight to the water, laughing as he held his hand beneath the soft flow of the waterfall.

'You mean the Zargons?' Lovell ventured as he lowered himself into a plush chair. The moment he had settled back, an adjutant presented him with a tall glass of fresh Zinca juice. It was only when he had taken his first sip that he noticed Clarence had been given a beer. Typical.

'Your escape from the Nebula Penitentiary would have been discovered within a few hours,' Zana explained. 'They'll be looking for you now.'

Lovell raised his eyebrows. 'You're saying the Zargons put me in The Neb?'

'I think Ro Silvari did their dirty work for them,' Zana nodded. 'The Zargons wanted you out the way. In just a few more days, the condition would have been permanent.'

Lovell swallowed. He knew she was right. 'But what was in it for Ro? Why would she double-cross me?'

Clarence squashed his empty beer can in a hairy fist. 'Why do you think?' He narrowed his eyes, pointedly.

'Payment?' Lovell mused.

'Think again.'

Lovell took a sip of his juice. Just how much would be enough to tempt Ro to betray him? The realisation hit him like a brick. 'She got my gold?'

'We think so,' Colonel Zana nodded.

'How? Rudy was the only one who knew its location.' Lovell turned to look at the huge robot.

'I kept the location a secret, sir,' Rudy thundered.

'Don't worry,' Lovell nodded. 'I believe you, Rudy.'

The robot's eyes glowed in response.

'There are many questions to which we don't yet know the answer,' the President interjected.

'Which reminds me,' Lovell said, placing his empty glass on the floor by his chair. 'I had a bit of trouble in The Neb with a guy named Gomo. He took an immediate dislike to me on account of my part in the last Zargon conflict. I soon put him in his place of course.'

Clarence noticed his friend was carefully avoiding his gaze as he spoke, a sure sign that there was more to the story than he was letting on.

'But he said something very interesting. He asked me a question that I had never considered and I had never heard anyone ask before. Not throughout the whole shebang on the Zargon asteroid.' The old captain leaned forward, determined to look the President in the eye. 'Why did the Zargons want to invade Kestra?' Lovell spread his arms wide. 'It's a good question. I mean, what was their game plan? What had Kestra ever done to deserve it?'

Colonel Zana looked to her president. He returned her gaze, his almond eyes searching hers. At last, he rose from his chair. Walking to the large, blank wall at the end of the room, the President pressed the palm of his hand against a panel in the corner. Lovell heard Jhy gasp as the wall seemed to disappear and be replaced with a view across the mountains of Estoran. Brakka Eagles soared gracefully beneath them, the sun catching the iridescent colours in their wings.

'Wow!' The boy ran to press his nose against the glass, his robot dog yapping at his heels.

'The Zargon home world is dying,' the President sighed as he gazed across the vista. 'For generations, it had everything we had; clean air, pure water, freedom. Then the Elites pushed to militarise the planet. They mined for minerals, they dug for ore. The processes they used polluted the air and tainted the water. Their people started to die. Rather than halting their militarisation programme, they ramped it up. At the same time, the Elites separated themselves from their people and imposed martial law. While they lived in high-rise homes above the toxic clouds, their water filtered and their air purified, the population below grew sick. And they looked at Kestra with envious eyes.'

'Why Kestra?' Clarence was as absorbed as Lovell.

The President turned back into the room. 'Colonel Zana, would you?' As he walked back to his chair, Zana took his place by the window. With a wave of her hand, the view beyond the glass was replaced by a star field. A blue-green planet spun slowly at its centre, five moons orbiting lazily around it. Lovell recognised it at once. Kestra.

The image froze and zoomed in. The picture was replaced by a computer animation showing a quarter of the planet removed. The crust and mantle peeled away, a section of the planet's core was exposed.

'Kestra is, as far as we know, unique in the galaxy.' Zana pointed at the swirling mass at the heart of her planet. 'It has a core of solid libidium, a highly active element that burns with a heat unknown in the universe. Thus, we have found it to be the perfect source for clean, safe energy.'

'Your whole planet is powered by its core?' Clarence was amazed.

Zana nodded. 'Two generations ago, we committed ourselves to drilling further than we have ever drilled before.' The animation showed a shaft being sunk from the planet's northern continent, through the outer rocky layers and down to the centre. 'We drilled down three thousand kilometres until we made contact with the core,' Zana explained as the animation continued. 'We then developed systems to mine the material and carry it to processing plants on our planet's surface. A tonne of libidium is sufficient to power a city like Estoran for decades. It is a clean, safe and cheap form of energy that has fed our planet for the last twenty years.'

Lovell let the air whistle between his teeth. 'Impressive,' he admitted.

The President nodded, gravely. 'The Zargon attack was a last ditch attempt to save their race,' he said. 'They planned to invade Kestra, subjugate our people and exploit the source of our energy.'

Zana took up the reins of the conversation. 'Our intelligence suggests that they intended to corale the indigenous population into camps in the ice regions, while the invading forces would have occupied our cities.'

'They must be desperate,' Clarence muttered.

'Indeed,' the President agreed. Lovell noticed that, rather looking angry at the implications, he looked sad.

'But, I don't understand,' Clarence said. 'If they have the tech to launch an attack of that size, why can't they replicate your idea with their own planet's core?'

'Because their planet has a core of ice,' the President replied. 'Cold, inert and ineffectual.'

'It's almost poetic,' Clarence commented, only to catch Zana's disapproving eye. 'Sorry,' he said, 'it's the philosopher in me.'

'And you, John Lovell, foiled that attack.' The President leaned forward in his seat. 'It's no wonder they wanted you out of the way.'

Lovell was thinking hard. 'But the fact that they did, would indicate they were about to try again.'

'You're right,' agreed Zana from the wall screen. 'Or rather, we think they're about to try *something else*.' She turned back to the control panel and waved her hand again. The image of the bisected planet was replaced with that of a cloud of debris, tumbling in space.

'Asteroid cluster?' suggested Clarence from his chair.

'We don't think so.' Zana passed her palm in front of the control panel. 'Watch.'

Before their eyes, a computer simulation showed what would happen if the disparate lumps of rock and dust were put back together.

'It's a moon,' Lovell exclaimed as he gazed at the barren ball of rock in the centre of the screen. 'Or it was.'

'If so,' interjected the President, 'then it's not one we've seen before.'

'We think it's a rogue,' Zana continued. 'Our scientists have calculated that it's not been seen in our system for at least a hundred thousand years.'

Lovell was amazed. 'What happened to it?'

'It was deliberately destroyed.' Zana had never looked so serious.

Clarence had joined the little party at the screen. 'You're sure?' he asked, resting on his knuckles.

Zana nodded. 'This was no natural disaster. The shatter pattern is the giveaway. And our instruments tell us those rocks have undergone stress from internal sources.'

'It was exploded from the *inside*?' Lovell was having trouble taking all this in.

In reply, Zana reached a palm towards the screen. She pinched her fingers together as if grabbing at the image, then swept her hand downwards. The moon revolved about its equator in response, until Lovell was staring down at its pole. There he saw a deep shaft had been sunk deep into the rock. It was perfectly round, its walls smooth and regular.

'Wait. There's a piece missing?' Clarence had raised himself up to take a closer look. 'Where did it go?'

'We don't know,' the President sighed. 'And that's the worry.'

'But you suspect the Zargons?' Lovell scratched his chin in thought.

'There's no other civilisation in the system that would have the capability.' Zana waved her hand to flick the screen off. 'We just don't know why.'

The image was replaced with the familiar view of the mountains of Estoran. Jhy gave a little cheer in response. He patted his lap to attract Dash's attention and, as the diminutive robot climbed into his knees, they both sat, gazing out at the soaring eagles. The little dog's mechanical tail wagged, happily.

'Okay,' breathed Lovell. Here came the sixty four million credit question. 'What's this got to do with me?'

The President turned his almond eyes upon him in a direct stare. 'You saved us once before, John.'

RICHARD JAMES

There was the use of his first name again. First Zana, now the President himself. Lovell was worried. He waved absently at the wall screen. 'You think that whatever happened to that moon is a direct threat to Kestra? How can you possibly know that?'

'As I said,' the President replied, 'there are many questions to which we do not have the answers.' His brow furrowed into a frown. 'And that is... most troubling.'

Lovell sighed. 'So, what do you want me to do? Go check out this moon?'

'No.' The President moved to the centre of the room, as if to indicate the conversation was about to take a more serious turn. 'I want you to go to the Zargon home world.'

Lovell's eyes grew wide as he looked at an equally astonished Clarence. Rudy, who had been conserving his batteries in a corner, sprung suddenly to life and stomped over to his companion.

'Perhaps my aural circuits are malfunctioning,' he boomed, 'but I could swear he said you're to go to the Zargon home world.'

'That's exactly what he said,' replied Clarence, shaking his head.

'Are you crazy?' Lovell gasped as he turned to the President. 'You said yourself, I'm a wanted man. You expect me to just waltz in without them noticing?'

The President raised a hand to placate him. 'You will have The Valiant at your disposal. That means you will be undetectable as you approach the planet. And she's quick, able to outrun any ship in the galaxy.'

'She's well armed, too,' Zana added. 'That should be all the protection we need once we make planet fall.'

'What do you want me to do once I get there?' Lovell knew that, despite his protestations, he was going to go. Of course he was.

The President walked towards him in a direct appeal. 'Find out what the Zargons are up to. And stop it.'

Lovell puffed out his cheeks and rubbed the back of his neck. Then he looked suddenly at Zana. 'Wait. You said once *we* make planet fall.'

'Of course,' Zana smiled. 'You don't think I'd let you go alone.'

Rudy stretched himself up to his full height. 'And I guess you're going to need some muscle,' he thundered.

'Thanks, pal,' Lovell replied.

72

'I guess I've got nothing planned for the next few days,' added Clarence. 'And I'd love to get my hands on The Valiant's flight controls. She looks a doozy.'

Zana laughed. 'She certainly is.'

'Lovell?' came a small voice from behind them. 'Dash and I want to play, too.'

Lovell looked down at Jhy, then squatted beside him. 'This ain't no game, kid.' He ruffled his hair. 'This is deadly serious.'

'Oh, we can do serious.' Jhy turned down his mouth almost comically, and Dash dropped his gaze to the floor in an attempt to look more sombre.

Lovell couldn't help but laugh. 'I guess you two have helped me out of more than a couple of scrapes in the past. But remember,' Lovell wagged a finger at the boy's face. 'I promised Dorita I'd look after you.'

Jhy threw his arms around Lovell's shoulders. 'And you've sure done a good job so far!' he beamed.

Lovell patted him gently on the back as he looked around the room at his motley companions. A Kestran Colonel, a talking chimpanzee, a demolition robot and a small boy with a metal dog. He wouldn't have had it any other way.

VII

HEART TO HEART

'So, how does it feel to be a fugitive?'

'About the same as it felt to be a hero.'

Lovell and Zana walked among the looba trees of the presidential grounds. Lovell relished the rare opportunity to amble away from the crowds. Here, if the President's gardeners and groundskeepers did recognise him, they were discreet enough to keep their thoughts to themselves. Zana had looped her arm through Lovell's as they walked. As much as he might have wished it meant something more, he knew it was simply an expression of companionship. He appreciated it, nonetheless, especially after everything they'd been through together.

Zana had bathed and changed into cooler clothes, taking the opportunity to relax a little before their mission.

'So, Lovell,' she purred as they turned down an avenue of broad-leafed shrubs, 'do you mind if we get a bit personal?'

Okay, thought Lovell. He'd been expecting this ever since Zana had rescued him from The Neb. If she had watched his trial, as she had claimed, he knew there was only one thing she would want to know. *Here it comes.*

'Sure,' he nodded.

Zana nuzzled closer to his shoulder. 'Who is Ro Silvari?'

Lovell took a breath. 'A friend,' he said. 'Or at least, she was. Actually, she was the wife of a friend.'

'Threep?' Zana let her gaze wander through a gap in the trees as they walked. She noticed a gang of danuby monkeys fighting over the low hanging fruit.

'I'd known Threep Silvari for years,' Lovell was saying. 'We'd run the spice routes together back in the day. Everything was a competition with him.' Lovell smiled. 'If I got a hundred credits for a haul, he'd get a hundred and one. I beat him once, of course.' He

75

was suddenly wistful. 'Threep Silvari was in love with a certain lady, but she was having none of it. He lavished her with shoma flowers, bought her the finest wines. Truth was, she was rather taken with a grease monkey from the boondocks. He was young, idealistic. Had nothing to offer such a beautiful woman, but still she fell for him.' Zana noticed Lovell's pace had slowed. 'And he fell for her, too.'

'Your wife?' Zana nudged him gently.

Lovell nodded. 'It was the start of something special, Zana. We were never apart. We grew into ourselves. Lived together, worked together, even joined the military together.'

'Did Threep forgive you?'

Lovell laughed. 'Of course! Trouble was, he was still consumed with love. It was as if, with Strella gone, he had to put it somewhere else.'

Zana blinked. It was the first time she had heard him mention her name.

'So he gave it to Ro.' Lovell guided Zana to a bench. She sat beside him, her legs brushing against a clump of *Flora Carillon*. They tinkled delightfully, adding an incongruous music to Lovell's story. 'When Strella died, I lost my mind with grief. I was literally no use to anybody. I was invalided out of the military and I went home to the one friend I had. Threep Silvari. He could see I needed help. He let me stay with him and Ro. Slowly, I emerged from the darkness. Threep could see I needed a new start. A way of earning a living. A reason to live. So, he gave me his ship.'

'The B156?' Zana smiled at the memory of Lovell's rickety Transporter.

'It wasn't much, but it was a lifeline.' Lovell swept the hat from his head, fanning his face with the brim to cool the sweat on his forehead. 'Yup, old Threep sure came through for me. I dare say I wouldn't be sitting here now if it weren't for him.'

'Then, it seems Kestra is in his debt, too.' Zana squeezed his arm. 'But, at the trial, Ro said you had stolen the ship.'

Lovell shook his head. 'I don't understand it.'

'And the video evidence?'

'Of me killing Threep? Never happened.' Lovell turned to gaze into Zana's almond eyes. 'You do believe me?'

'Without a shadow of a doubt,' Zana replied, her voice thick with emotion.

'I mean, I know he was killed at the local market, but it sure as hell wasn't me.' Lovell slapped his hat back on his head. 'As far as I remember, I was thirty light years away.' Zana didn't have to know the details. 'I knew nothing about it until I got back.'

The Colonel took his arm again as they rose to continue their walk. Once through the avenue, they were rewarded with a view of Estoran beneath them. A waterfall fell to their right, sparkling in the light of the Kestran sun. It emptied into a large pool almost choked with luscious plants. As Lovell watched, a carnivorous juke flower opened its petals to snap at a passing insect.

'How was Ro after that?' Zana asked. 'It couldn't have been easy for her.'

'She was a changed woman,' Lovell replied as they strolled around the pond. 'Desperate even. She made a move on me once or twice, but there's only ever been one woman for me. And, of course, they never found Threep's killer.' He shook his head. 'I can't imagine she would actually believe it was me.'

Zana thought for a moment. 'I guess whoever doctored that footage would have had access to the original recording. *They'd* know who it was.'

'I guess,' Lovell agreed. 'I'll look them up just as soon as I've saved Kestra from the Zargons.' He winked at Zana, teasing. 'Again.'

VIII
BEST LAID PLANS

'**S**he handles as smooth as she looks,' Clarence beamed from the flight deck of The Valiant.

As the craft lifted off from the launch pad, Lovell noticed he could barely hear the hum of the engines. 'Sweet,' he muttered. Secretly, he missed the rough and tumble of his old ship. He remembered how he could feel every bump and jolt through the old Transporter's controls, how he'd have to wrestle with her and cajole her, to bend her to his will. Now, *that* was flying.

'She's practically flying herself,' the chimp exclaimed. He leaned back in his pilot's chair, folding his long arms behind his head. 'I had no idea space travel could be so relaxing.'

'Cute,' Lovell hissed, reluctantly.

'And take a look at this.' Clarence flicked a switch on the dashboard and the floor beneath Lovell's feet dissolved away.

'Woah!' Lovell exclaimed, stamping his feet against the deck. It still seemed firm enough.

'Ain't that cool?' Clarence laughed.

Lovell looked down to see the Kestran capital dropping away beneath them. In moments, they were above the cloud layer and he could see the curve of the horizon ahead.

'It's a projection,' Colonel Zana explained from the co-pilot's seat. Having changed back into her military uniform, she looked ready for anything. 'Each tile on the outer hull contains a tiny camera. The interior is a wrap around screen and the data is displayed in real time. Oh, and it's three sixty.' Reaching out to another switch, she toggled it round to alter the view. Now, Lovell was staring up above him as the blue of the Kestran atmosphere gave way to the blackness of space. He had to admit it was impressive stuff. 'I could engage all the cameras at once if you want,' Zana smiled.

'No thanks,' belched Lovell. 'I've not long had my lunch. I'd like to keep a hold of it.'

Zana laughed as she switched off the screen and turned to the navigation panel. 'I'm just checking our coordinates.' A three dimensional image appeared above the dash. It showed a sun blazing in the centre, with Kestra in an orbit that kept it directly opposite the Zargon home world. A small, flashing circle indicated The Valiant's position. Various areas in space were highlighted with different colours. 'Spatial anomalies,' Zana explained. 'Asteroid fields, meteor clusters and dust clouds. The kind of thing we should really be avoiding if at all possible.'

'That's an impressive bit of kit,' Clarence whistled. He turned to Lovell. 'If we'd had one of those in the Transporter, we could have saved a hell of a lot in repairs.'

Lovell harrumphed. If they'd had one of those in the Transporter, it would have practically doubled the ship's value.

'Permission to engage the ion drive?' Clarence's fingers were itchy.

'Go ahead,' Zana nodded. 'The nav computer's plotted a course already.'

'Great!' Clarence didn't need telling twice. His hairy hands danced over the dashboard before, finally, hovering over a large, red button. Bunching his fingers into a fist and turning to Lovell with a grin, he slammed his hand down hard. The effect was a resounding anti-climax. Whereas the engines had, only moments before, been emitting a gentle hum, they now fell completely silent.

'Well, what were you expecting?' Zana asked off her friends' confused looks. 'A flash of lights? Big whooshing sound?'

'You gotta admit, it's kinda disappointing,' Lovell frowned. The ship didn't seem to be moving at all. He had no doubt that it was pitching and reeling through the eddies of space but, from the inside, the dampening circuits gave the illusion of a calm stillness.

Zana puffed out her cheeks in exasperation. 'Some people are just too hard to please.'

'How long we got?' Lovell asked.

Zana turned her attention to a small screen. 'We'll be at the Zargon home world in thirteen hours.'

Lovell eased himself from the cabin seat with a nod. 'I'm going to check on Rudy and Jhy.'

The giant robot was squatting on the floor, his eyes narrowed in concentration. Before him was a stack of rectangular blocks arranged into a tower. Taking turns, he and Jhy were removing a block at a time, each of them trying to prevent the tower from falling as they did so.

'I haven't played Bunja since I was a kid,' Lovell smiled as he approached.

When Rudy spoke, it was not with his usual voice, but Lovell recognised it, nonetheless. 'It is simply a question of imposing your will on the power of your actions.'

'Sumara?' Lovell gasped. 'Rudy, how did you do that?'

Rudy turned his great head and blinked his visual receptors. 'Sumara is only gone in a physical sense,' he growled.

'What other sense is there?' Lovell was taken aback.

Rudy tapped his chest where, if he were human, his heart would be. 'The spiritual sense.'

Lovell's jaw hung open.

'Sumara's spirit lives in Rudy,' Jhy confirmed. 'His shulka is within him.'

'Shulka?'

Rudy reached out to the pile of blocks. 'Everything he ever saw, everything he ever *was*, is within me.' His huge fingers closed around a wooden brick towards the bottom of the tower. Slowly and deliberately, he pulled the block from its place. He did it with such delicacy, Lovell noticed, that the tower stood as strong as ever.

'John Lovell,' came Sumara's voice again. 'You see how a piece may be removed and yet the tower remains?'

Lovell felt himself nodding in spite of himself.

'So, even though I am gone, the team you assembled remains. Strong and dependable.'

Lovell shook his head, unsure quite what to believe.

'Doubt is good, John Lovell,' Sumara's voice continued. 'Questioning the truth can lead to true enlightenment.'

It sure sounded like something Sumara would say. Was he really alive in Rudy's mechanical brain? He remembered the robot saying that somewhere in his memory was a file marked 'Sumara'. Perhaps that was it. His thoughts were interrupted by Dash yapping and scurrying about at his feet.

'No, Dash!' cried Jhy. 'Be careful!' Clearly upset at being ignored, the robot dog had decided that enough was enough. He ran between Rudy and the boy, his metal tail wagging furiously. Rudy reached out to swat the dog away, but not before he had careered through the tower, sending blocks flying around the hold.

Jhy laughed as Rudy cradled his head in his hands in mock despair. 'Come here you scamp!' The boy sprang to his feet to give chase, following his excitable pet through the hatch and onto the flight deck.

'Hey, Jhy,' Clarence beamed from the pilot's chair. 'Come to see where the action is?'

Jhy scooped a bleeping Dash into his arms and looked around him. 'What's that?' he asked, pointing at the three dimensional nav control. Ahead of the flashing dot representing The Valiant, he could see a highlighted area just ahead of them.

'Ah,' replied Zana, enigmatically. 'I guess we've got time to take a look. Lovell!' she called, 'Come see.'

The old captain appeared in the doorway, a bemused look on his face.

'Take a seat,' Zana commanded. 'You too, Jhy.' As Lovell and the boy took their places, Zana leaned over to Clarence. 'Power down the ion drive.'

Clarence stabbed at a series of buttons and the engines resumed their previous hum. 'We're in normal flight,' he announced.

'Great.' Colonel Zana reached out to the toggle for the viewer circuits and one whole side of the ship seemed to drop away.

Lovell gripped the sides of his chair as he felt himself suspended in space. He had to remind himself it was nothing more than a projection from the thousands of tiny cameras on the outside of the ship. He heard Jhy gasp beside him and followed his gaze to see a wrecked hulk hanging in the vacuum.

'A Zargon battle cruiser,' Clarence whistled from the pilot's seat.

Lovell swallowed. 'It's still out here?'

'It's the last,' said Zana. 'We dismantled the others before the Zargons could salvage them. This one'll be next.'

Clarence leaned on the controls to move The Valiant closer. Lovell peered up as they entered the huge hangar area. Above them hung the rusting remains of a laser cannon.

'When we destroyed the asteroid, the destruction signal was sent to the whole fleet via a communication wave,' Zana was explaining. 'They detonated almost instantaneously.'

'So, there was no chance to abandon ship?'

Zana flashed Lovell a stern look. 'Do you think they would've given us a chance to abandon Kestra?'

Clarence took The Valiant out via a hole in the ship's hull. The little craft looked smaller still against the sheer size of the battle cruiser. Climbing higher, The Valiant circled the huge ship's bridge, now a tangled mass of metal and deck plates. The little party looked on in silence.

'Why do people do bad things?' Jhy asked, suddenly.

Lovell rubbed the back of his neck. 'Lots of reasons, kid. But mainly, they're born that way or something makes 'em that way.'

'What made the Zargons bad?'

Lovell thought for a while. 'Desperation,' he said, quietly. He turned to Zana. 'Okay,' he said. 'Let's get outta here.'

Zana toggled the screen off then nodded to her simian co-pilot. 'Next stop, the Zargon home world,' she said, as Clarence jabbed at the controls. He brought a fist down on the button but, instead of the engines falling to an eerie silence as they had before, they gave an ominous whine. Suddenly, the little ship was buffeted left and right. It rose and fell as if caught on a wave. For the second time, Lovell found himself clutching his seat.

'What's happening?' he yelled above the noise.

Clarence was jabbing frantically at dashboard. 'Nothing!' he shouted back.

'Sure doesn't feel like nothing.' Lovell reached for his seat's restraints and snapped them across his chest.

'And it doesn't *look* like nothing.' Jhy was pointing to the three dimensional display. It showed the flashing dot that represented The Valiant blinking on and off. Sometimes it would disappear entirely, only to reappear in another part of space altogether.

'How is that even possible?' Zana was punching at the nav controls. 'I've lost control of the ship!'

'But there's *nothing* there,' Clarence protested. 'Literally nothing. Every scan's coming back negative.'

'Then it's a ship malfunction,' Lovell hissed. The cockpit walls were beginning to twist and buckle.

'Nope,' replied Clarence, his fingers flying over the controls. 'Everything's operating within usual parameters.'

'You're kidding, right?' Lovell felt his stomach in his mouth as the ship pitched and rolled.

'We're going to have to put down somewhere.' The colour drained from Zana's face as she tried to make sense of the situation.

'But where?' Clarence cried. 'We're not in one place long enough.'

'We're going to have to make a break for it the moment we see an opportunity.' Zana called.

'But that's crazy.' There was a note of panic in Lovell's voice. 'Like jumping off a moving monorail as it passes through a station.' He noticed neither Zana nor Clarence were quick to contradict him. 'And we could end up anywhere in the solar system.'

'We don't have a choice, Lovell,' Clarence replied. 'Much more of this and The Valiant will be ripped apart.'

'But you said there was nothing out there!' Lovell was bewildered. 'How can you run away from nothing?'

'Ready?' Zana grit her teeth.

'Ready,' Clarence replied.

As the ship rocked all around them, the chimpanzee listened hard to hear Zana's command above the noise of the engines. The Colonel was watching the holographic projection intently. Just as the dot representing The Valiant blinked into existence at a point in space that she felt would be safe enough, she leaned forward to engage the landing procedures. 'Now!'

In response, Clarence cut the engines. The ship seemed to fall through space. Lovell was sure that, had he not been strapped in, he'd have been pinned to the ceiling. In fact, Dash *was* pinned to the ceiling. The little robot dog was yapping happily in response to the forces that held him there.

'This is fun!' squealed Jhy from beside him.

'There!' Zana was pointing through the cockpit window to a cloud-covered planet below. 'Set her down there.'

Lovell's eyes widened. 'Can't we just continue on to the Zargon home world now we're free of the *nothing*?'

Clarence shook his head. 'We've sustained damage to just about every system.'

'But we don't know what's down there,' Lovell protested. 'We don't even know if there *is* anything down there.'

'Scans are indicating a breathable atmosphere and gravity comparable to Kestra. There's organic life, too. And water.' She squinted at the screen. 'Lots of water.'

'Okay,' scoffed Lovell, rolling his eyes. 'But apart from *that*, we don't know what's down there.'

The ship was buffeted by high winds as they descended through the cloud layer. Jhy raised his hands and gave a scream of delight as if they were riding on a car at a theme park.

'I've lost vertical thrust,' Clarence reported. 'I'm gonna have to glide in.'

'Great,' hissed Lovell.

'Come on, Lovell,' the chimpanzee grinned. 'This is just like old times.'

The ship dropped again and Lovell got the sense they were losing altitude quickly.

'I've got her,' Clarence assured him. 'Look out for a suitable landing spot once we're through the clouds.'

Zana toggled a switch. The whole of the underside of the ship seemed to disappear. Lovell swallowed. It was as if there was nothing between the soles of his boots and the planet below. Rain lashed against the craft as they descended. Although there were still gusts strong enough to tip The Valiant's wings, the ride was noticeably smoother. Lovell noticed the clouds weren't quite so turbulent the lower they dropped.

'Look!' cried Jhy, excitedly. Looking down, Zana saw a rocky outcrop looming out of a swirling sea. Aside from the small island, there was nothing more as far as she could see.

'Well,' she shrugged, 'looks like that's the best we can do.'

'And just in time, too,' Clarence added, grimly. 'I've just lost power to the ailerons.' The ride was suddenly more uncomfortable, with every bump and drop in altitude seemingly magnified tenfold. 'I gotta switch to manual.' The chimp stabbed at a button to reveal a pair of joysticks. He grabbed each one in a hairy fist and leaned his weight into them both.

'You got this, Clarence,' Lovell hissed, more to reassure himself than anyone else.

The island loomed large beneath them. So large, that Lovell thought he could reach between his knees and touch it.

Through the lashing rain, Clarence could see a narrow plain between two peaks. It was draped with lush vegetation, which he hoped would cushion their landing.

'Wait,' Lovell cautioned him, 'you don't know what's beneath all that foliage.'

'Sheesh,' mocked Clarence. 'And to think, on Kestra, you're worshipped as a hero.'

Lovell took the hint and decided to let his old companion concentrate on doing what he did best; getting them out of trouble.

IX

TERRA FERMA

Krick stood beneath the wide frond of a palm, sheltering from the rain. Over his shoulder hung two bokbeasts, their tongues lolling. They weren't as big as he would have liked, but recent events had affected all natural life on the island. He knew the other hunters of the tribe would have been stalking similar quarry. Hopefully, between them, they would have caught enough to feed the village for a few days. Adjusting his haul, Krick turned to begin the walk back. Just as he'd taken his first step, his eye was drawn to a disturbance in the clouds above. A strange object was dropping from the sky. It was like a bird but much bigger and its wings were rigid. Behind it, a dark smudge of smoke mingled with the storm clouds.

Krick crouched low behind the trunk of a tree to watch as the object plummeted towards the ground. As it passed, he was sure he heard an irregular whining noise. The mysterious bird seemed unstable, pitching and rolling as Krick had often seen the boats on the sea. Stepping forward for a clearer view, he saw its wings clip the edges of the taller trees before plunging deep into the canopy. Then, all was still. Krick took a deep breath to calm his racing heart, dropped his heavy quarry, then sprang into the undergrowth to go and alert the villagers to this strange, new arrival.

'Everyone okay?' Clarence unclipped his restraints and spun round in his chair.

'Well done, Clarence,' Lovell smiled. 'I never doubted you.'

'Sure,' Clarence laughed.

'You okay, Jhy?' Zana snapped off her restraints and knelt down next to the boy.

He looked at her with wide eyes, an enormous grin on his face. 'I'm just fine,' he beamed. 'And so is Dash!' He lifted his arms to show the robot dog crouching on his lap, his visual sensors blinking with excitement.

Lovell turned to see Rudy stomping through the hatch from the cargo hold. 'Did I miss something?' he rumbled.

'Rudy!' Jhy cried, jumping from his seat. 'We crashed!'

'Hey!' Clarence interjected. 'We did not crash.' He caught Lovell's eye. 'We landed creatively.'

Zana laughed as Lovell clapped the chimpanzee on his shoulder. 'Okay,' he said, looking around him. 'What now?'

'Well,' Colonel Zana began, 'we should be safe outside, but I guess we need to think about repairing the ship if we ever want to leave.'

'Is that even possible?' Lovell thought of the way the ship seemed to buckle and twist as it was tossed around in space. And then there was that *creative landing* Clarence had mentioned. He doubted The Valiant could have come out of that unscathed.

'It's all superficial,' Clarence said with certainty. Whether it was genuine certainty or not, Lovell couldn't be sure. The chimpanzee was looking at the various dials and readouts in front of him. 'It looks like it was a cascade failure, which means it had one initial cause that rippled through the whole ship.' He scratched his chest absently as he thought. 'If we can fix that, everything else should fall into place.'

'Great.' Lovell leaned over the dash. 'Can we get a message to Kestra? Maybe they can send help.'

'Comms are down,' Zana reported.

'Of course they are.' Lovell looked resigned. 'We also need to know what the hell it was we ran into up there. You okay to stay here with Rudy and make a start on that, Clarence?'

The chimpanzee nodded.

'I will be glad to help,' Rudy announced.

'Zana, you, me and Jhy can take a look around outside. See what's what.' Lovell reached for a small laser pistol. He threw one to Zana, too.

'Sure.' Zana was heading to a locker hidden in a bulkhead. 'Then I guess we're gonna need these.'

Lovell was taken aback. 'What are you looking for? Survival rations?'

'Nope,' Zana twinkled. Reaching into the locker she pulled out several pairs of rubberised boots. 'It looks filthy out there.'

The outer door opened with a hiss of hydraulics as the ramp extended onto the jungle floor. As Lovell descended, Jhy's robot dog zoomed ahead into the undergrowth. The old captain stopped to take a deep breath of the sweet, damp air. 'What are we looking for?' he called back as Colonel Zana appeared behind him.

'Anything that'll be of immediate use,' Zana replied, her almond eyes scanning the foliage. 'We've got good shelter in the ship, but we're going to need food and water. I wasn't exactly counting on being stranded on a strange planet.'

'Fair enough,' Lovell smiled.

Stepping from the ramp, Lovell found himself walking on soft soil. The rain had become a mist that hung in the air. As he walked, a thin film of moisture developed on his face and forearms, in no time at all, his shirt was soaked with sweat.

'It's humid,' he said, taking his hat from his head to wipe his forehead with the back of his hand.

Soon, they were plunging into thick undergrowth, though Lovell was sure he noticed a few trodden paths among the tangle of roots and rotting leaves. Ahead of them, he could hear the sound of rushing water.

'There's fruit on some of the trees.' Zana was pointing up into the canopy. Looking up, Lovell could see clusters of bright orange and purple fruit about the size of a Zinca.

'We can send Dash to cut some free,' Jhy exclaimed excitedly.

'I don't know,' cautioned Lovell. 'Look closer.' He gestured up towards the fruit.

'Ew,' Jhy exclaimed. 'What's that?' He had noticed the fruit was scarred. A greyish sludge oozed out of great welts in their flesh.

'Best to be careful, eh?' Lovell concluded.

'Good idea,' Zana agreed. 'We'll take them back to The Valiant for analysis before we eat them.' She winked at Jhy. 'Better to be safe than sorry.'

As they pushed on through the jungle, they suddenly found themselves standing on a precipice. The view was dizzying. To their left, a vast waterfall poured from a wall of rock studded with minerals. Down it plunged to a deep pool of seething water. The noise was so loud that Lovell had to shout to be heard above it.

'There's our water!' he yelled.

'Providing it's safe to drink,' Zana cautioned.

They stood for a moment, surveying the scene, then turned back to the ship. As they passed a tall tree they had been using for a marker, Lovell leaned against its trunk and held up his hand.

'Anyone else noticed how quiet this place is?' he asked, peering into the jungle around him for signs of movement.

Zana and Jhy were listening, too.

'No birds, no animals scurrying in the undergrowth,' Lovell whispered.

Zana nodded, thoughtfully. 'The jungles on Kestra are teeming with life. So should this one be.'

A sudden gasp interrupted the conversation. Looking down, Lovell saw Jhy had his eyes tight shut. He recognised it as a sign that the boy had initiated psychic contact with his robot dog.

'Danger,' Jhy breathed, hyperventilating. 'There is danger!'

Lovell didn't wait to act. 'Let's get back to the ship,' he hissed. Just as he straightened himself up from the tree trunk, there was a rustling in the bushes around them.

'Quiet, did you say?' Zana rasped, suddenly alert.

The rustling was coming from all around them. Suddenly, the foliage parted to reveal a woman dressed in leather and fur. She was armed with a long wooden spear, sharpened to a fearful point. Next to her, a man emerged from behind a broad leafed shrub. He was similarly dressed and had a bow and arrow pointed ominously at Lovell and his friends. Next to him, another man appeared, then another woman. Each had a weapon raised, each had murderous intent in their eyes.

Both Lovell and Zana drew their laser pistols. There was a sudden crack of air and they felt their guns snatched from their hands. To either side of the little party, two children stood with whips. As Lovell rolled his eyes, the children both bent to the ground and retrieved the weapons.

Lovell looked slowly around. They were surrounded. Peering closely, he saw that many of them had signs of trauma on their skin. One woman had great blisters on her forearm, another had dark shadows under her eyes. The final man to appear held a net back before him. With a gasp, Jhy saw it contained a captive Dash. He was kicking his robot legs to no effect, held fast in the twist of rope and twine.

'No!' the boy screamed. Lovell took him by the shoulder to restrain him.

'Not now, kid,' he soothed.

'I guess we should signal our surrender,' Zana whispered, raising her hands above her head. Unarmed as they were, she knew they'd be no match for the weapons currently aimed at their heads.

Lovell followed suit, nudging a tearful Jhy to do the same.

Slowly, the circle of men and women parted to reveal a path through the jungle. The woman that Lovell had seen first gestured with her spear.

'Move,' she growled.

The village was set in a clearing between the trees. From the rumble of water, Lovell guessed they were only a short walk from the waterfall. Platforms had been built in the trees, reached from the ground by ladders and ropes, and Lovell could see men, women and children leaning against the wooden railings to peer down at their captives. To one side, a sheer chalky cliff rose above the trees. There was a cave mouth at its base that had been worked up into an elaborate entrance. Lovell noticed strange carvings around the doorway. Trees and shrubs, animals and birds had all been etched into the rock. Ironically, he thought, there was probably more wildlife carved around that doorway than he'd seen on the planet so far.

The little party was pushed past puddles of water towards a fire that burned in a central pit. The remains of an animal hung from a spit. Beyond this, stood a large, wooden throne. It had been fashioned to represent a huge beast rising up behind the occupant. Its front paws were the arms, its hind quarters curled beneath to provide a base. The woman sitting beneath its open jaws appeared no less fearsome. She looked ancient, her face lined and pitted with age. A fur robe hung from her shrunken frame. Small she may be, thought Lovell as they were pushed before her, but it was clear she was in charge. He noticed her neck was covered with an angry looking rash.

'Krick was right,' said one of the men who had captured them. 'They are outsiders. They bring death to our village.'

His assertion was greeted by a cacophony of noise from the trees. The tribespeople were banging on the trunks with short lengths of wood. Lovell noticed how thin they looked. They exhibited the same rashes and blisters he had noticed before. Some raised their fists or shouted threats from their platforms. Others threw rotten fruit.

'They dropped from the sky in a shining bird,' a young man called above the din. 'I watched them fall from the clouds.'

This must be Krick, thought Lovell. He looked as fierce as the rest of his tribe.

'We mean you no harm,' Zana was saying, carefully.

The two children placed the recovered laser guns at the old woman's feet.

The man with the net stepped forward and emptied it at the ancient woman's feet. 'This belongs to the boy,' he reported. 'It is like no animal I have seen before.'

'It's just a robot dog,' Lovell explained, before realising that very few of those words would have made any sense at all. He turned to Jhy. 'Why is he so still?'

Jhy tapped his forehead. 'I have sent him to sleep so he comes to no harm.'

'We didn't mean to come here,' Zana was explaining to the old woman. 'Our ship crashed. We just need to repair it and we will leave.'

'A ship?' the old woman repeated. 'From the sky?'

'Yes,' Zana replied. 'Like a ship of the sea but…' she thought how best to explain it. 'The stars are our waves.'

'They lie!' came a shout. 'Nothing can fly that high.'

'If they did, they would scratch the sky!'

Again, the air was full of the sound of wood on wood.

The old woman held up a hand to quieten the throng. As the crowd grew still, she leaned forward on her throne. 'Why do you starve us?'

Lovell looked around him. Again, he was struck by how thin the tribespeople looked.

'Why do you poison our water?'

Lovell pointed beyond the trees. 'You *have* water.'

'It is corrupt,' the old woman snapped. 'You have poisoned it from your home in the mountains.'

'We don't live in the mountains!' Lovell protested.

Colonel Zana was more circumspect. 'There is another tribe in the mountains?' she asked.

'They pretend they do not know!' called an old man from the edge of the clearing.

The old woman appeared to be thinking hard. 'Your dress and language are strange. You are outsiders. You are not to be trusted.'

'We have hurt no one,' Zana asserted again, holding her hands wide. 'You have our weapons.'

'Unfortunately,' Lovell grumbled beneath his breath.

'They need no weapons to pollute our water!' shouted a woman from a platform in the trees. She held a baby in her arms. It was so weak that it was barely moving.

'Nor poison our animals!' came another voice. It was greeted with another round of noise as sticks were banged on trunks.

Zana raised her voice. 'We have done neither of those things!'

The old woman struggled to her feet. There was a respectful silence from the tribespeople.

'The gods have sent the outsiders to us,' she intoned, 'so that we may be rid of them.'

'What?' Lovell looked worried. 'What do you mean by that?'

'Tie them up!' the woman commanded. 'If they are put to death, the waters will run clear again. The gods have willed it!'

In the melee, Lovell noticed Dash was still lying by the fire, quite still.

'Jhy,' Lovell whispered to the boy next to him, 'can you connect with Dash?'

Jhy nodded.

'Do what you can,' Lovell continued. 'But make it quick.' He looked at Zana. 'The ship,' he hissed as they were manhandled across the clearing. 'We've got to get word to Clarence and Rudy.'

'How?' Zana whispered back. 'None of us thought to bring comms.'

Lovell grit his teeth in frustration. 'Will we ever learn?'

Each of the outsiders was marched to their own tree and secured against it, their hands forced around the trunk and tied with a vine.

'We need to stall them,' Zana rasped. 'A distraction of some sort.'

Lovell wondered how. 'I'm all ears.' In front of them, a line of archers stood with their weapons raised, ready for the word from their leader. Lovell noticed that Dash, unseen by the villagers, had risen to his feet. Sniffing the air, he looked about him.

'No,' Lovell heard Jhy whisper, 'there are too many of them. Find another way.' The boy had his eyes squeezed shut, a sure sign that he was in psychic communion with his robot dog.

Lovell saw the dog slip behind the villagers and head towards the cave mouth. He twisted his head to Zana. 'I think we might be about to get that distraction.'

All around them, the villagers had fallen to their knees. Holding their arms out and their palms to the sky, they started to intone an ominous prayer to their gods.

'Oh, tree gods,' the old woman moaned above the noise, 'we offer these outsiders that you might take the poison from the water, make the animals well and the birds sing.' The prayer grew louder as the woman began to sway. She held her hands to the sky as if she might touch the clouds. 'Their lives in exchange for the bounty you have taken from us. One life for the water, one for the animals and one for the birds.'

The prayer stopped and the villagers rose to their feet. They stared in absolute silence as the old woman gave the command.

'Raise your bows,' she called.

Lovell grit his teeth. 'Zana,' he moaned, 'If this is the end –'

'*If?*' Zana interjected, her almond eyes wide with fear.

Lovell met her gaze. 'I just wanna say. It was fun.'

Zana smiled back in spite of their predicament. 'Yeah,' she beamed. 'It was, wasn't it?'

'Take your aim,' came the old woman's voice again and the line of archers readied their bows. The prisoners took a breath to steel themselves and waited for their fate. Lovell screwed up his eyes in anticipation. *I hope it's quick*, he thought.

'They shall drop from the Tree like the Fruit.'

The old woman gasped at Jhy's sudden interjection.

'They shall drop like the Fruit, as messengers from the Gods,' Jhy continued. Lovell dared to open his eyes, only to see Jhy still had his tight shut. He saw the woman was suddenly unsteady on her feet.

'Lower your bows,' she said, her lip trembling. The archers looked confused. 'Lower them!'

Their weapons lowered, the villagers looked to their leader for an explanation.

'What's going on?' whispered Zana.

'Beats me,' Lovell replied. 'But I think it might be working.'

'They shall be sent at the hour of most need,' Jhy was saying. Lovell thought it was almost as if he was reading. 'And they shall be as the bokhound to the Lost Hunter.'

'They are from the tree gods!' The old woman fell to her knees then stretched herself out on the dirty ground. 'Forgive us!' she was wailing. 'You are sent from the gods to save us, as the fruit drops from the tree. As the bokhound to the Lost Hunter.'

'Who are they?' called a villager from the crowd. Lovell recognised him as Krick, the young man who had witnessed their crash landing.

'The boy speaks sacred words known only to me and to the gods,' the woman explained, fitfully. 'They are written in the Temple for my eyes only.' She stretched a bony finger towards the cave mouth in the rock. 'It is a prophecy. They have come to save us!'

With gasps of shock, the villagers took their lead from the old woman, prostrating themselves before their prisoners.

'That's right,' called Zana, sensing their way out. 'We can help you!' Suddenly uncertain, she turned to Lovell for reassurance. 'Can't we?'

'Sure!' Lovell joined in. 'Like the, er, *bokhound to the Lost Hunter*.' In response, the villagers prayed again. This time, Lovell noticed, it sounded like a prayer of thanks. 'Now,' he continued, bravely, 'the messengers of the tree gods need someone to untie them.'

'I feel uncomfortable,' Colonel Zana admitted as she passed Lovell his laser gun and holstered her own. She looked round the interior of the temple. Candles had been lit so that the little party could read the tablets of wood that hung from the walls.

'Oh, yeah?' Lovell teased. 'Did you feel more comfortable with a dozen arrows pointed at you?'

'They think we're gods,' the colonel replied.

'No,' Lovell corrected her, 'they think we're *messengers* from the gods. Just like it says in their holy tablets.' He waved at the carvings around them. 'Look at this one here.' Lovell pointed to an illustrated panel showing a sad looking tribesman being guided back to his village by a wolf-like creature. 'The bokhound and the Lost Hunter.'

'Are we really part of a prophecy?' Jhy asked, full of wonder.

'I dunno, kid,' Lovell admitted. 'Seems to me, if any prophecy is vague enough it'll come true eventually.' He ruffled the boy's hair. 'We're just lucky that Dash saw it when he did. If you hadn't seen this writing through his eyes, we'd be full of holes by now.'

'It doesn't bother you that we're taking advantage of their beliefs?' Zana was running her fingers over the carvings.

'Hey,' Lovell admonished her. 'We haven't forced them to believe it.' He couldn't help but feel a little guilty under Zana's stern gaze. 'We just *let* them believe it.'

'And, who knows?' added Jhy, scooping his robot dog into his arms. 'Perhaps we might be able to help them.'

Zana turned to face him. 'We've got to get to the Zargon home world, Jhy. We can't hang around here for long.'

Lovell shrugged. 'We've got some time on our hands while Rudy and Clarence fix the ship.' He walked back to the entrance, jamming his hat back on his head as he talked. 'Seems to me, we got a prophecy to fulfil.'

'Okay,' Lovell announced. 'We're gonna help you.'

There was a roar of approval from the crowd.

'You say your animals and birds have died, leaving you hungry.'

'The water is polluted!' came a woman's voice. Lovell watched as she stepped forward. It was the young mother he had seen earlier, watching from a platform in the trees. 'It is why we collect the rain.' She pointed to the puddles around the settlement. Lovell could see that they were lined with animal skin to stop the rain from seeping away. 'It turns bad within days,' the young mother continued, 'and it rains so rarely.'

'Because the water is bad,' added one of the men Lovell remembered from the line of archers, 'we dare not drink it. It makes us sick. The animals and crops are dying.'

'When did all this begin?' Zana asked.

The old woman blinked. 'Since the night of the lights in the sky.'

'Lights?' Lovell echoed.

'Twelve nights ago,' the woman continued, 'lights fell from the sky to land in the mountains. Since then, the water has been poisonous to us.'

Lovell turned to face the towering mountains in the distance. 'Then that's where we'll begin,' he said. 'But first, I need to introduce you to some friends.'

X

THE EXPEDITION

The villagers stood, open-mouthed. Before them, stood an eight-foot mechanical man and a beast in a clean, white tunic.

'This is Rudy and Clarence,' Lovell explained. 'They fell with us, like Fruit from the Tree.'

'Huh?' Clarence grunted, confused.

'Just roll with it,' Lovell said, under his breath.

'Oh, okay. Sure.'

'They will help us in our mission. They are your friends.'

Rudy dropped to one knee in an apparent attempt at humility. 'Friends,' he boomed.

The effect was immediate and probably not the one he'd hoped for. The sound of his voice was enough to send many of the villagers scurrying for the trees.

'He speaks like thunder!' quivered a young man.

'Yeah,' Lovell conceded. 'You get used to it.'

'He is strong,' Zana called, flexing her arms in demonstration.

'And I'm the brains of the outfit,' Clarence added. 'Without me, they're nothing.'

'The beast speaks!' the young man shouted in disbelief.

'Hey!' Clarence replied, clearly wounded by the remark. 'I'd like to hear you discuss the finer points of military philosophy, then we'll see who's the beast.'

'The five of us are a team,' Lovell continued with a smile. 'And we can help you.'

There was a murmur of excitement and, slowly, the crowd drew nearer. Lovell bowed low to the old woman on her throne. 'With your permission, your ladyship?' The woman smiled and waved her assent. 'We will go to the mountains and find the source of the pollution. We will find it and stop it.'

The air was filled with the sound of wood on wood. Looking around him, Lovell saw the villagers still on their platforms were hitting the tree trunks with their wooden batons. This time, he was pleased to see, it was a gesture of approval.

'And if we can't?' Zana asked the old captain so the villagers wouldn't hear.

Lovell met her gaze. 'Then we've got a lot of explaining to do.'

Following some sort of ceremony during which the old woman had appeared to bestow her blessings on the enterprise, Lovell, Rudy, Jhy, Zana and Clarence had been shown to the river's edge. A team of villagers had brought them five wooden boards. After a quick demonstration, they were handed over along with a paddle each and the little party were invited to take them out into the water. Lovell gripped the sides of his board as he struggled to his knees, the rush of water threatening to capsize him.

'Need a hand there?' Clarence asked from near the centre of the stream. Daring to look up, Lovell saw that he had taken to his board like a chimp to water.

'I thought chimpanzees were afraid of getting wet?' Lovell sneered.

'I'm not your average chimpanzee,' Clarence retorted. Paddling lazily through the water, he had planted his feet firmly on the wooden platform and was slicing confidently through the foam.

'I'll be okay once I'm up,' Lovell lied.

'If not,' called Jhy from his board, 'I can tie a rope and tow you.' Dash had activated his mini thrusters and was buzzing excitedly ahead of them, keen to get on with their adventure.

'I don't need any help,' Lovell insisted as he wobbled to his feet. For a moment, it looked like he might just make it, too. Just as he reached down into the water with his paddle, however, he lost his balance and pitched overboard. To screams of delight from the usually more restrained Colonel Zana, Lovell felt himself struggling against the tide. Determined not to swallow any of the polluted water, Lovell fought to find his footing on the river bed. He caught sight of the villagers on the riverbank as he sank beneath the waves. Some looked horrified at his predicament, others slapped their sides with laughter.

Reaching out for his board, Lovell struggled to heave himself out of the water. Suddenly, he found himself being lifted clear of the river and deposited safely on board. Looking round, he saw Rudy standing waist height in the waves.

'Don't mention it, sir,' the giant robot rumbled. Having decided he could do without a board himself, Rudy strode happily off through the seething water.

'Okay,' Zana called when Lovell looked as stable as he ever would be. 'We need to go if we're gonna get there by nightfall.'

'I'll be fine,' Lovell reassured her as he leaned unsteadily into the current. 'As long as you don't mind *which* nightfall.'

The going was hard. The further they paddled, the stronger the current became.

'Why couldn't the mountains be downstream?' Lovell panted as he dug in with his paddle.

Zana shot him a pitying look. 'Think about it,' she said.

All around them, the jungle became more dense. Occasionally, they would spot an animal lying dead at the river's edge, a victim of the poison in the water. The further they paddled upstream, the more they saw trees and shrubs looking rotten and withered, their fruit inedible. Lovell could see why the villagers were so desperate.

Zana led them towards the quieter sections of the river but still they had to work hard to make progress. Once or twice they stopped for breath by the river's edge, all except for Rudy who would insist on wading ahead to look for a safer route. During one such hiatus, Lovell noticed Clarence was looking more tired than the others. His chest rose and fell as he took great gulps of air.

'Guess I'm just outta shape,' he reasoned as Lovell caught his eye. 'Gotta cut down on those Fazuna Bars.'

At last, just as the sun was setting behind the trees, they rounded a bend to see the end in sight. The river was flowing from a crack in the mountainside. The rock around it had been smoothed over the millennia, and it glistened with seams of minerals.

'That's the source of the river, right ahead of us.' Following Zana's gaze, Lovell saw the water emerging from a bubbling spring in the ground, deep inside the mountain.

'Let's ditch these boards and do the rest on foot.'

'Great,' breathed Lovell with relief. 'I thought you'd never ask.'

'Jhy,' Zana commanded. 'Send Dash ahead to see what he can see.'

'Sure thing!' exclaimed Jhy. His robot dog yapped excitedly, clearly happy to oblige.

As the little party laid their boards on the pebbly shore, Lovell turned to his chimp companion. Clarence was wheezing and groaning as he rested against the cave wall.

'How you feeling, Clarence?'

Suddenly self-conscious, the chimpanzee beat his chest in a show of strength. 'Never felt better,' he said, none too convincingly. Lovell smiled in response, but couldn't hide how concerned he was.

'There's a wall,' Jhy said suddenly, his voice echoing in the empty space. 'A wall of rocks.' He had his eyes tight shut as he spoke.

'Is that what Dash can see?' Zana asked.

Jhy nodded. 'Up ahead.'

Rudy looked interested. 'Walls of rock are what I do best.'

Lovell laughed. 'Okay big guy, take it easy. Let's take a look first, huh?'

He led the way to the back of the cave, past the bubbling spring that was the source of the river. With Zana and Jhy following in his wake, he called to the giant robot. 'Hey, Rudy! Can we get a little light in here?'

Rudy nodded his great head and the cave was illuminated by two beams of light from his eyes. Lovell gasped as the minerals in the wall shone like stars in the night sky. Patches of slimy moss had made their home in the notches and cracks. Above him, pitch black stalactites hung from the cave ceiling. At last, he found himself standing before a wall of irregular shaped rocks blocking any further exploration. Looking down, he saw Dash perched on a ledge, his ears twitching.

'Good boy,' said Lovell, almost involuntarily.

'Ready?' rumbled Rudy from beside him. With a grinding of tiny gears, he bunched his huge hands into fists, ready to pummel at the rock face.

'Steady, Rudy,' Lovell smiled. 'Let's just loosen a few first, then send Dash through to take a look.'

If a robot could look crestfallen, then that's exactly how Rudy looked.

'Think of it as an opportunity to practise your dexterity,' Zana said, which seemed to cheer him up. As Rudy lumbered forward, the Colonel turned to Lovell. 'This isn't the result of a rock fall,' she said, thoughtfully. 'Looks like they were placed here purposefully.'

Lovell nodded. 'And recently, too.' He pointed at the rocks that were lit by Rudy's shining eyes. 'The moss hasn't had a chance to grow.'

Zana could see he was right. The spongy moss that grew all around the cave wall was nowhere to be seen on the rubble. 'So, I guess there's someone or something behind it that doesn't want to be found.'

'Well,' Lovell shrugged. 'We just found them.' He nodded to Rudy. Gingerly, the demolition robot reached out to the rocks and began to tease one out of the wall. Lovell could tell he was holding back the urge to simply smash through. Rudy manipulated the huge boulder as if it was no heavier than a pebble, released it from its position and placed it on the ground. It left behind it a gap just big enough for a robot dog to fly through.

'Okay, kid,' Lovell whispered. 'Let the dog see the bone.'

Jhy closed his eyes as Dash rose into the air on his mini thrusters. 'Go get 'em boy,' Jhy encouraged him. Pressing his mechanical ears back against his head, Dash made his way through the gap in the rock wall.

There was a pause. All eyes turned to Jhy, waiting for his report. 'The passageway opens into a basin,' he said at last. 'It's open to the sky.'

Zana frowned in thought. 'A natural caldera?'

'And there's a ship,' Jhy said, excitedly.

'A ship?' Clarence was sitting on a ledge nearby, resting. 'What sort of a ship?'

Jhy squeezed his eyes tighter shut. 'Go closer, Dash,' he whispered. 'Go on, boy.'

'The lights in the sky,' Lovell said. 'Could they have been a ship landing?'

Zana nodded. 'According to the old woman, that's when the pollution started.'

'The ship is small,' Jhy announced. 'Looks damaged.'

'A crash landing?' Lovell mused.

'There's a sign on the side,' Jhy continued. 'An insignia.'

'What does it say?' Clarence had risen unsteadily to his feet.

Jhy took a breath and reached out involuntarily. His fingers caught a hold of Zana's arm and squeezed. He opened his eyes, a look of terror on his face. 'It's Zargon.'

'Zargon?' wheezed Clarence. 'What are *they* doing here?"

Lovell looked at Zana. 'They can't be looking for me. They've been here for twelve nights.'

Zana agreed. 'Unless we were forced here in what *looked* like an accident.'

'They don't look like soldiers,' Jhy interjected, his eyes closed again.

'You can see the crew?' Lovell rested a hand on the boy's shoulder. 'How many are there?'

'Four,' Jhy replied. 'One of them is injured.'

Lovell nodded. 'I like those odds,' he smiled, holding up his gun in readiness.

'They are wearing uniforms,' Jhy continued, 'but they're not military.'

'Can Dash get any closer?' Zana asked.

'Careful boy,' Jhy whispered to his dog. 'Get as close as you can, but look out.'

Lovell gnawed at his lip in anticipation. If they weren't soldiers, then who were they? And what were they doing on this strange planet?

'They're scientists!' Jhy exclaimed at last.

'Shh!' Zana put a finger to his lips. 'You're sure?'

'They have badges on their uniforms,' the boy explained. 'Science Corps.'

'Zargon scientists?' Clarence looked as confused as everyone else. 'Why would Zargon scientists be hiding out on an evolutionary backwater?'

Lovell shrugged. 'There's only one way to find out.' He turned to Jhy. 'You might want to tell your dog to take cover. Rudy?' With a whirring of servos, the robot stretched himself up to his full height. 'Do your thing.'

Rudy looked as delighted as any robot could possibly look. 'Yes, sir,' he rumbled. He took a step back.

'Er, Lovell,' Zana interrupted. 'Shouldn't we think about what we're gonna do once we're through?'

But it was too late. Rudy had launched himself at the rock, his arms spinning furiously in front of him. His hands had become two huge shovels, scooping great boulders from the pile as if they were made of cardboard. Once or twice, Lovell was sure he saw sparks as Rudy's metal fingers scratched against rock. Gone was the delicacy he had employed when dressing Lovell's wounds on The Valiant. Now, he was what he was made to be. An R49 demolition robot.

The cave was soon full of dust. The noise was deafening as Rudy threw the loose rocks behind him. Lovell wished he had Jhy's psychic connection to his dog. He had no idea how the Zargon scientists behind that wall were reacting. Had they rushed to find their weapons at the first sign of trouble? Were they, even now, lined up with their guns aimed at the emerging robot, ready to open fire? He suddenly felt completely unprepared. He really should have listened to Zana's plea to pause and think through the possibilities.

Rudy had cleared all the rocks from his path. As Lovell, Zana and Clarence stepped carefully into the cavern beyond, they were greeted by the sight of four figures, cowering against their ship. Zana and Lovell raised their guns.

'Please,' stammered an older man with a bald head and full beard. 'This was all my idea. Don't punish them,' he gestured to his frightened colleagues. 'Take me.'

'No,' interjected a stern young woman. 'We all agreed to this. We're all responsible.'

A third person spoke up. He was older than the rest and his uniform hung loosely from his shoulders. 'Do what you like to us,' he said bravely. 'You'll never break us.'

Colonel Zana held up her hands. 'We're not who you think we are,' she said gently. 'And we're not here to capture you.' As she stepped into the light, the four scientists had their first view of her distinctive almond eyes.

'She's a Kestran!' The bearded man almost spat the word.

'What are you after?' asked the young woman. 'Revenge?'

Lovell hung back in the shadows. If they were Zargons, then they would almost certainly recognise him. He had to remind himself that, as far as the Zargon Empire was concerned, he was a wanted man.

'We're here to help the inhabitants of this island,' he growled. 'Things haven't been going great for them since you arrived.'

The older man looked surprised. 'Inhabitants?' He scratched his chin. 'We've tried to keep ourselves to ourselves while we fix our ship.'

'You crashed?' Zana asked, moving slowly towards their vessel.

'We've come quite a way,' the bearded man explained. 'This little ship wasn't really up to it.'

'Why here?' Zana persisted.

The man narrowed his eyes. 'I could ask you the same question.'

Finally, Lovell stepped into the light. He holstered his gun as he saw Zana do the same. 'We were forced down.' He could see recognition in the scientists' faces. 'We ran into something strange up there,' he raised his eyes skyward, 'and wound up here.'

The fourth scientist, older than the others, had struggled to her feet. Lovell noticed blood on the leg of her uniform. 'I know you,' she hissed.

Lovell shrugged. 'I get that a lot.'

'You're John Lovell,' she sneered. 'Well, well. John Lovell, a Kestran woman, a giant robot and a little orphan boy. The only thing that's missing is a talking chimp and we'd have the full set.'

'You were saying?' Clarence followed Lovell into the cavern, trying his best to hold himself upright.

The wounded woman laughed. 'Oh, boy. If we handed you over to the Zargon Empire we could all retire on the proceeds.'

Zana was thinking. 'But you won't, will you?' She looked around her. 'A ship, totally unsuitable for a planetary expedition. A small team of scientists with no scientific equipment. And you're not armed.' She narrowed her almond eyes. 'It's almost as if you had to leave the home world in a hurry.' The colonel folded her arms, as if waiting for an explanation.

The Zargon group stared back at her for a while, uncertain how to proceed. Then, finally, the bearded man stepped forward.

'I'm Stahn,' he said. He pointed to the older man beside him. 'This is Tal.'

The stern woman joined him. 'I'm Vern,' she said, suddenly not so stern. She gestured to the wounded scientist. 'This is Glin.'

'What happened to your leg?' Lovell asked.

Glin looked down at her blood soaked uniform. 'I was caught under one of those rocks when we built the wall. It doesn't seem to want to heal.' She nodded to the pile of debris, all that was left of Rudy's demolition. 'It took us longer to build it than for him to tear it down.'

The scientists led Lovell and his team over to the ship and beckoned them in. Zana stole a questioning look to Lovell, who nodded that they should follow. As he walked painfully up the ramp, Clarence noticed a crack in the ship's hull. An ominous, green glow was emanating from the circuits and systems beneath.

'Space fatigue,' Stahn shrugged. 'And we don't have the tools to fix it.'

Zana shivered as she looked around the cramped craft. She wondered if she was the first member of the Kestran military to walk on board a Zargon ship.

'We spend most of our time in here,' Glin announced. 'For the light and the warmth.'

Lovell nodded. It was definitely warmer in here than outside in the cavern. The ship's interior was divided into small bays containing beds and medical equipment.

'And we have enough supplies for now.' Boxes littered the floor. Lovell saw packets of dried food and high-energy juice. It was clear they weren't going to last long. 'We grabbed what we could,' Glin explained, almost apologetically. 'We had to dump the medical supplies to make room. Otherwise, I'm sure we could've fixed my leg.'

'Did you build that wall to keep the villagers out?' Clarence asked, lowering himself down on a low seat with a wince of pain.

'We didn't know anything about any villagers,' Stahn said. 'We didn't have time to do a scan for resident life forms.'

Lovell undid a button on the collar of his shirt. 'Then if you didn't build the wall to keep the villagers out...' He let the point hang in the air. There was another silence.

'They'll be after us,' Glin said, at last.

'Who?'

'The Elite.' Glin looked at her colleagues. They stared back with caution in their eyes. 'These people might be our only way out of here,' she hissed.

'That's right,' Lovell nodded. 'We might.'

'You mentioned your ship was forced down,' said Stahn.

Lovell nodded. 'Er, yeah.'

'Is it still in working order?'

Lovell's eyes flicked to Clarence. The chimpanzee shook his head.

'Yeah,' Lovell lied. 'Sure.'

'You see?' Glin smiled at her fellow scientists. 'They can get us out of here.'

'To where?' grumbled Tal. 'Kestra?'

'Why not?' Glin implored. 'There's nothing for us now back on the home world.'

'You would be welcome,' Colonel Zana reassured him.

Lovell was keen to hear more. 'So, what happened on your home world? Why are you running?'

Stahn stood to gaze out of the cockpit window, deep in thought. He was clearly weighing up just how much he should divulge.

'We were all assigned to… a *project*.' Stahn had turned and was eyeing his colleagues carefully. 'We didn't agree with the direction our Elite was taking but, on the Zargon home world, agreement isn't sought. It is our place to serve. No questions.'

Tal took up the story, his old eyes looking sadder than ever. 'We worked in isolation. We had no idea what we were contributing to until the test.'

Lovell raised an eyebrow. He didn't like the sound of that. 'Test?' he growled.

Now it was Vern's turn.

'It seems we were part of a team developing a deadly new weapon,' she said. 'We were based on the home world, but the test took place thousands of light years away.'

'What test?' Lovell repeated. He sensed a reticence in the scientists.

'We destroyed a rogue moon.' Stahn's bottom lip was trembling. 'It was devastating.'

Zana remembered the briefing she and the President had given Lovell. 'How?' She was almost afraid of the answer.

'The device drills down to a planet's core.'

'With a perfectly aligned plasma cannon,' said Vern. Lovell thought he caught a note of pride in her voice.

Tal sat down and leaned forward, his elbows on his knees. 'Then the core is extracted via super strength grappler line.'

'As to why,' interjected Glin. 'We have no idea.' The other scientists nodded in unison. 'Above our pay grade.'

Zana turned suddenly to Lovell. 'The debris,' she said aghast. 'That was the result of the Zargons' test.'

Lovell whistled between his teeth. 'That's one hell of a weapon.'

'Hell is about right,' said Stahn, sadly.

'The four of us decided we couldn't be involved any further,' Stahn said. 'We had to get out.'

'Where is this weapon now?' Zana asked, quietly.

'Hidden,' Tal replied.

Lovell's eyebrows rose. 'How do you hide a thing like that?'

'We created a gravity well around it,' Vern volunteered. 'That was the last thing we worked on before we left the home world.'

'Our supervisor, Leutna Jaht, was murdered due to a technical failure.' Vern looked sad. 'It was not a price *we* were prepared to pay.'

'It wasn't easy to get out,' said Tal. 'We had to commandeer this ambulance vessel and load our supplies without being suspected.'

'We even changed our fuel to zetron radiation so we weren't so easy to trace.' Vern seemed proud of herself again.

Clarence was suddenly alert. 'Did you say *zetron* radiation?'

Vern nodded. 'It has a super high energy.'

Clarence looked alarmed. 'But zetron radiation is deadly if it interacts with organic matter.'

Vern shrugged. 'So is any radiation, given time.'

'I saw a crack in the engine casing,' Clarence mused aloud. 'Could it be…?'

'What?' Lovell knew that look in his chimp companion's eyes.

'Lovell,' Clarence began, 'it's not the water that's poisoning the village. It's the radiation.'

Zana frowned. 'Zetron radiation?' She looked around her. 'Then how come the scientists aren't suffering as much as the tribespeople?'

'They said they spend most of their time in the ship,' Clarence explained. 'The interior is protected from the engines by the radiation shields. It's only when they're outside they would feel the effects.'

'Then, that's why my wound isn't healing,' mused Glin.

'How come we don't feel it?' Lovell asked.

Clarence pulled up a sleeve on his tunic. 'Speak for yourself.' As he parted the hair on his forearm, Lovell could see a blister developing on Clarence's skin. 'Looks like chimps are especially susceptible.'

Zana pulled Jhy close to give the boy some comfort.

'We had no idea.' Tal looked appalled at the implications.

'How many villagers are there?' asked Stahn.

'A hundred or so,' replied Lovell. 'And they're all suffering. The wildlife, too. Trees, plants, they're all dying. They thought it was the water.'

'But it's us,' said Glin, sadly. 'It's our fault.'

'What can we do?' Stahn asked in desperation.

'Our ship has a tractor beam,' said Zana. 'We could tow your vessel clear of this planet.'

Lovell looked doubtful. 'That would all depend on whether we can get it working.'

Stahn was aghast. 'You said it was in working order!'

Lovell shrugged. 'It will be,' he promised, 'just as soon as Clarence gets it fixed. Eh, Clarence?' He looked over to his chimp companion, only to see him slumped, unconscious, in his seat.

XI

INFILTRATION

Under-Leutna Mev had assembled the best marksmen that were available to him. He had commandeered a stealth craft from the Zargon home world and now he and six crack soldiers descended through the atmosphere of the planet Yoba. Mev was amazed and not a little impressed that the scientists had made it this far. He knew they had only managed to steal an ambulance craft that was usually used for short hops. They had made one mistake, however. It seemed they had swapped fuel to evade detection by Zargon scans but that had not been enough. Everyone working on the Doomsday Device was, as a matter of course, suspected. Their communications were tracked and monitored every hour of every day. They had been careful, but not careful enough. One of the scientists, an older man called Tal, had been unable to resist a vidcall to his sister. He had spoken elliptically, but the Zargon Communications Unit had been listening. Seeking to reassure his sister, Tal had sent the coordinates of his destination in the audio stream accompanying his call. Because of that, Mev had never been in any doubt where the traitors had been heading.

Yoba was in orbit on the Kestran side of their shared sun, thousands of light years from the home world. No doubt their ship would be in a bad way, Mev smiled to himself. That meant the scientists' chances of escape would be lower than he'd anticipated. With any luck, this would be a quick in and out. A surgical strike. Not that he'd tell Grand Leutna Shavan that, of course. He had already decided to dress up his report a little, whatever the actual outcome. Mev knew the price to be paid for failure, but he also knew success was rewarded. And the greater the success, he hoped, the greater the reward. So, his report would detail just how brave he and his men had been, how they had overcome insurmountable odds and how he, Under-Leutna Mev, had proven himself an exemplary leader. Calm under pressure but relentless in his pursuit of the traitors. That should please the Grand Leutna. Mev was already looking forward to taking his place alongside the Zargon Elite. The alternative made him shiver. Shavan's threats to his family should his mission fail were not idle. He looked around the cabin of the craft as the pilot made ready for their landing. The soldiers were indistinguishable from each other in their shiny black flight suits and helmets. They looked tensed for action, their Heat Exchange Guns resting on their laps. Mev snapped down his visor as the ship descended into the tree canopy. The door hissed open and a ramp extended onto the jungle floor.

'Okay,' said Mev over comms. 'You know who we're looking for. Show no mercy. The Grand Leutna isn't interested in having them back alive. Their bodies will do.'

The soldiers nodded smartly and stomped down the ramp. Just as he felt the soft vegetation beneath his boots, proximity alarms flashed on his Heads Up Display.

'Halt!' he snapped.

His visor was transmitting the locations of at least a dozen figures in the trees. Far too many to be the scientists. Slowly, the figures stepped from the undergrowth. Mev saw a motley collection of primitives dressed in furs and leather. Each of them had a weapon of sorts, from spears to bows and arrows, and they were pointed straight at Mev and his men. A woman with a spear was the first to speak and also, ironically the last.

'More strangers,' she growled. 'You bring nothing but trouble.'

Good, thought Mev. *So the scientists are here.* And that's all he needed to know.

'Fire!' he commanded. Before the primitives had time to react, the soldiers had swung their HE Guns from their shoulders and opened fire. Jets of flame spurted from the guns' rear exhausts as latent heat was sucked from the atmosphere and turned to ice bullets. The soldiers raked the tribespeople with their deadly ammunition, the bullets slicing into flesh and bone. Even those that turned to flee were mowed down in a vicious hail of ice.

The Under-Leutna's HUD showed their life signs fading. He smiled to himself and snapped on his comms. 'Find their village,' he rasped. 'The traitors may be there.'

With their guns still raised, the soldiers made their way slowly through the undergrowth, scanning the ground for previously trodden paths. 'This way!' called the lead soldier, her hand in the air. The troupe followed her beneath dense, low hanging palms, pushing the leaves away with their hands as they passed. Just before they entered a clearing, the squad leader raised her hand and the soldiers fanned out and took cover.

'What is it, Brunt?' Leutna Mev asked as he made his way over to crouch beside her.

'It's their settlement, sir,' she replied quietly into her comms. 'Sending you visual.' With a tap of her helmet, the soldier sent Mev's HUD an image of what she had seen.

Mev nodded. 'Looks like that's the place.'

'We've got maybe a hundred hostiles.' As Brunt spoke, various figures flashed red on Mev's display. 'More than half of them are in the trees on platforms,' Brunt explained, 'family units and children mostly. They don't seem to be expecting an attack.'

'Any sign of the scientists?' Mev asked.

'It's impossible to tell,' Brunt replied. 'There's a cave structure at the edge of the village. Our scans can't penetrate through the rock.'

'The perfect place for them to hide,' Mev mused. 'I'll leave it to you, Brunt. Go in hard.' The Under-Leutna retreated back to a sturdy tree trunk, the better to observe the unfolding mission.

'Squad,' he heard Brunt announce over comms. 'Be ready.' She held up an open palm and waited until she had her team's full attention. Then, when she judged they were poised for action, she clenched her fist and pulled her arm down swiftly. *Go.*

The effect was immediate. The soldiers, still crouched low behind their cover, unleashed a stream of bullets from their HE Guns. Before they realised what was happening, the villagers were strafed with ice. Those on their platforms fell dead to the ground or lay slumped against the trees. On the ground, people ran for cover as best they could. A team of three soldiers pressed forward, turning their guns to engage their port exhausts as flamethrowers. Fingers of fire licked at the wooden buildings. Sheets of flame set the trees burning. As Mev watched, he saw several of the tribespeople writhing on the ground, their skin blistering as they clawed at their burning clothes. Finally, a wooden chair in the centre of the settlement was set alight, but not before its occupant, a frail old woman, had been raked with ice.

At last, all was quiet, and the Under-Leutna stepped into the clearing. The attack had been so swift and so deadly, he noticed, that none of the villagers had even had the time to reach for their weapons.

'The cave is clear,' said Brunt over comms as she approached. 'Seems to be some kind of temple.'

Mev frowned as he looked around the smouldering remains of the village. 'Fan out,' he snapped. 'They have to be somewhere.'

XII
PARADISE LOST

'I think they call this *going with the flow*,' Lovell smirked as he pushed off from the stony shore. This time the little party sat on the wooden boards, their legs dangling into the water. Behind them, they each had a scientist as a passenger. Jhy squealed as the current took them swiftly away from the mountain. He and Stahn, who sat directly behind him, barely had to paddle at all. Dash, meanwhile, was living up to his name, flitting this way and that on his mini thrusters.

Zana cast a look behind them as Rudy brought up the rear. As before, he paddled through the water, the waves lapping around him just beneath his great chest. Clarence's limp form lay in the robot's arms, held safely above the spray.

'Can you save him?' asked Vern from behind her. She was trying to steer their way through the swell with a paddle.

'We have medical supplies aboard our ship,' Zana nodded. 'He'll be fine as long as we can get there in time.'

'Then you'll be able to fix Glin's leg, too?' Vern glanced across the river to where Glin was balanced precariously on Clarence's board. As she had it to herself, she had stretched her wounded leg out in front of her, desperate to keep it dry.

'I think so,' Zana nodded. 'We'll at least be able to clean it up and give it a new dressing. If she needs any further treatment, we'll have everything back on Kestra.'

Zana heard Vern snort from behind her. 'And what sort of welcome do you think we'll get on Kestra?'

'A cautious one,' Zana admitted. 'But you'll be treated fairly under the Galactic Conventions of Conflict.'

'The Zargons don't subscribe to the Galactic Conventions,' said Vern, warily.

Zana allowed herself a smile. 'Then it's lucky that we do.'

'We'll need to fix The Valiant before we go anywhere,' Lovell called above the noise of the water. 'I don't know how far Clarence got,' he added sadly, 'but I think he's done all he can for now.'

'We have restored power,' rumbled Rudy. 'We were rebooting the systems when you asked us to accompany you.'

'Okay,' called Lovell, impressed with their progress. 'So with any luck, we'll be good to go.'

'But go where?' asked Tal from behind the old captain. 'You mentioned you were thrown off course when you crashed here, but where were you going?'

Lovell frowned. He daren't tell the scientist that they were bound for the Zargon home world. 'You don't want to know,' he breathed.

'Hey!' Jhy's voice cut through the noise of the river. 'Look there!'

Lovell looked ahead to where Jhy was pointing. A column of dark smoke rose from the trees. From the amount of time they had spent on the river, he guessed where it was coming from.

'The village,' hissed Zana as if to confirm his suspicions. 'What do you think has happened?'

Their conversation was interrupted by a sudden slapping sound from the river, then another. Tal clutched at his shoulder. Lovell noticed blood escaping between his fingers. Looking towards the riverbank, he saw a figure ducking behind a twisted trunk.

'That's what happened,' he said as he drew his laser pistol. 'Concentrate your fire on that tree.'

Levelling their guns at the riverbank, Zana and Lovell let rip a volley of laser bolts. They fizzed through the air to tear at the tree trunk. Lovell saw the figure behind it suddenly twist and fall.

'Hold it,' Lovell commanded. 'Let's get to the bank. We're sitting grawbs out here.'

Rudy was the first ashore. Laying Clarence's limp body against a mass of tree roots, he stomped a few paces into the undergrowth, his great head swivelling this way and that in search of danger. Paddling furiously, the rest of the little group made for the water's edge. Once there, Colonel Zana sprang to the body they had felled by the tree. If the tight black flight suit it wore wasn't enough, the insignia on the helmet confirmed the figure's identity. 'Zargon,' she announced.

'Then they found us.' Stahn looked downcast.

'Of course they did,' muttered Tal. 'It was always only a matter of time.'

Vern looked nervously about her. 'But how?' she asked. 'We were so careful.'

Glin shook her head, sadly. 'Not careful enough.'

'Sorry to interrupt the navel gazing,' Lovell snapped. 'But this guy was clearly not alone.' A small light was flashing on the soldier's helmet. 'And right now, his suit is transmitting his exact location to the rest of his squad.'

No sooner were the words out of his mouth, than a hail of ice bullets whipped through the undergrowth. Some ripped into the trees, shredding their bark as if they were made of paper.

'Down!' yelled Zana as she dropped to the ground. Jhy gave a yelp of fear as he dived behind a clump of thick vines. Dash scuttled beside him with a whimper, his ears flattened against his metal head. But it was too late for Glin. Hampered by her wounded leg, she took a bullet to the back as she struggled towards cover.

'Glin!' yelled Vern from behind a fallen log. But she could see it was too late.

'Where are they?' hissed Zana. She and Lovell had scooted behind a broad leafed shrub on their knees and elbows. Now, their guns were drawn.

'Well,' Lovell retorted. 'The one place we know they're *not* coming from is the river.' He squinted into the trees. 'I'll concentrate on our left flank, you take the right.'

On a silent count, the two friends squatted back to back and fired into the undergrowth. The air was a fizz of ice and laser fire. Lovell saw movement from the corner of his eye. Having moved Clarence to safety behind a rocky outcrop, Rudy was rushing to their aid, his huge feet causing the earth to shake beneath them.

'I'll be your cover,' he boomed. 'Sir.'

Standing between the Zargon soldiers and their quarry, the giant robot seemed to increase in size. With a whirring of servos, he puffed out his chest and spread his arms wide. Ducking behind one of the behemoth's legs, Lovell could hear the ice bullets rebounding off his metal armour. He reached round to let off a volley of laser fire.

'Get behind Rudy!' he called over his shoulder. 'We need to get to our ship.'

Zana was at his side now, leaning round the robot's legs to return fire.

'And bring Clarence!' Lovell added.

Stahn leaned over to hoist the chimpanzee over his shoulder, then moved to cower behind the robot. As he did so, he saw Tal twist in the air. A bullet had struck his shoulder. As the force of the impact flung him into the air, he was struck again and again. Blood spattered his scientist's uniform. He fell to the ground with a sickening thud, his life seeping away into the leaf matter around him. Vern and Stahn looked at one another, aghast.

'We've got to move, Rudy!' Lovell called above the din.

'Yes, sir,' the robot rumbled. He took slow, lumbering sidesteps into the undergrowth, shielding the remaining survivors from the hail of gunfire. Jhy had joined them with his pet dog. Dash gave a sudden bleep and rose into the air, his mini thrusters blazing.

'No, Dash!' called Jhy. 'It's too dangerous!' But Dash ignored his pleas. As the boy watched, he sped into the canopy above the attacking Zargons and disappeared.

'I'm sure he can look after himself, kid,' Lovell assured him as he let off another series of laser bolts. A Zargon soldier fell from the cover of the trees, blood pouring from a wound in his chest. As a colleague ran to his aid, Lovell hit him, too. The force of the laser spun him round a full three hundred and sixty degrees, before the second soldier fell on the first, both of them quite dead.

'How many do you think there are?' Zana shouted in desperation.

'Two less than when they arrived!' Lovell called back. Despite his grim expression, Zana was sure she saw a twinkle of mischief in his eyes.

The little party crouched low behind Rudy as he moved through the trees towards The Valiant. Jhy could just make out the ship's gleaming hull through the foliage.

'Will we be safe there?' he asked.

'Once we're in with the door shut behind us,' Zana reassured him, 'the ship will keep us safe.'

'Hopefully, long enough for us to get it fixed,' Lovell added under his breath. A withering look from Zana told him to keep his thoughts to himself. Even in the heat of battle, she lost none of her capacity to keep him in check. In truth, he liked her for it.

'Look out!' Vern gave a shout as she moved to protect Stahn and Clarence. A Zargon trooper had skirted round them to approach from behind, his HE Gun spitting ice. Before Rudy could spin round, Vern had taken a bullet to the hip.

'We're surrounded!' Lovell yelled, firing into a knot of fallen branches where the soldier had dropped for cover. 'We've got to move quicker, Rudy!'

As the Zargon rose to fire again, he was suddenly felled by a large rock crashing onto his head from above. His gun spat ice randomly into the trees as he fell to the ground, his skull crushed beneath the weight of the boulder.

'Yay!' called Jhy. 'Go, Dash!'

Looking into the canopy, Lovell could see the small robot looping the loop in triumph, his front claws retracting now they had released their load.

'Good boy!' Jhy yelled to his pet. But his joy was short lived. Just as Dash pulled out of his celebratory dive, an ice bullet clipped him on the nose. It was enough to send him spinning towards the ground, a shower of sparks fizzing from the gash in his head. Jhy reached out and caught him in his arms.

Just as Rudy reached the clearing where The Valiant stood, its hull glistening in the tropical sun, the Zargon weapons fell silent.

'Wait,' said Lovell, suddenly concerned. 'They've stopped shooting.'

'Do we make a run for it?'

Lovell thought fast. 'We may have no choice.' No sooner were the words out of his mouth, than a sheet of flame erupted around them. 'They've changed tactics,' Lovell yelled as he ducked. 'They must be getting desperate. They know we're winning!'

Zana shielded her eyes as the trees around them erupted into a ball of flame. 'It doesn't *feel* like we're winning,' she confessed.

'Winning is simply a matter of not thinking like you're losing,' Rudy boomed.

'When did he get so philosophical?' Zana blinked.

'It's a long story,' Lovell sighed. 'Let's get to the ship.'

Rudy's gears whirred and hissed as he prepared himself for the final effort to reach The Valiant. As he strode into the clearing, he bent to one side. Seizing the moment, Lovell let loose a flurry of laser bolts. Another Zargon soldier fell to the ground, his body catching fire in the flames of his HE Gun. His screams were cut short by an ice bullet to the head. Rather than watch him die in agony, one of his fellow soldiers had chosen to offer him a quick death. Having dispatched his colleague, the soldier knelt on one knee to steady his gun against his shoulder. Looking around, Lovell saw that Stahn was dangerously exposed. And if Stahn was exposed, so was Clarence.

As the soldier squeezed on his trigger, Lovell noticed Rudy move in a blur. Plucking at a tree trunk twice his own width, he uprooted it as if it were a sapling. Swinging it over his head like a huge cudgel, the mighty robot advanced on the Zargon trooper. Panicking, the soldier fumbled with his gun. Rudy gave a great mechanical roar as he came within striking distance. The Zargon opened fire, his HE Gun spewing a hail of ice onto the robot's great chest. Seemingly oblivious to the onslaught, Rudy swung the tree before him, catching the trooper and flinging him against a jagged boulder. His gun rattling harmlessly away, the Zargon rolled to the ground, his body broken.

Taking advantage of the chaos, Lovell, Zana, Jhy and Stahn ran up the ramp to safety. Vern limped after them, clutching desperately at her wounded hip.

As Lovell ushered her in, he leaned out on the ramp to fire at a Zargon in the trees. A flash of sunlight on the trooper's visor had been enough to give away their location, and now they paid the price. The soldier slumped first to their knees and then to the ground, a scorch mark on their neck showing where the laser had hit.

Stahn lowered Clarence onto a medbed and, looking around to get his bearings, started searching through nearby lockers for medical supplies.

'Raise the ramp!' Zana yelled from the flight controls.

'No!' Jhy screamed. 'Not without Rudy!' He had placed Dash on a table in the hold and now stood clutching Lovell's sleeve.

Looking out the door, Lovell could see the giant robot stomping across the ground to the ramp. His attention drawn to the demolition robot, the old captain didn't notice another Zargon step from the trees. This one wore a different uniform and a badge indicating a position of authority.

'Lovell!' Jhy cried, pointing as the Zargon reached for his utility belt. Lovell raised his laser gun as Under-Leutna Mev snapped a light grenade from his belt and pulled the pin. Throwing his arm forward, he released the grenade into a graceful arc that could only end at one point; in the entrance hatch to The Valiant.

'Down!' Lovell yelled as he flung Jhy to one side. Seeing the boy crouching behind a sturdy bulkhead where he landed, Lovell threw himself onto Clarence's medbed, covering as much of the chimp's inert body as he could. Even as he waited for the blast, he felt a sense of relief that he could feel his old friend was still breathing. *Funny*, thought Lovell, *you can find hope in the most desperate situation*. He blinked. He shouldn't have had the time to think that at all. By now, the cabin should have been ablaze with a scorching, searing light. Daring to look behind him, Lovell saw something that made his jaw hang slack in amazement. Some distance away, to the Under-Leutna's right, Rudy was standing quite still, his arms raised. His eyes glowed a fierce red and his head was angled as if he was leaning into a strong wind. The object of his focus hung in the air, just before the entrance hatch. The Under-Leutna's light grenade. Lovell noticed that the pin was depressed, preventing its detonation. He glanced at Rudy and saw the robot's fingers were curled around an invisible object. The Zargon's face was a mask of disbelief, but Lovell had seen this before. Not from Rudy, but from his old friend Sumara. The mystic had been able to control physical objects through the exertion of his will. Now, it seemed Rudy could do the same. Did Sumara really live on inside the metal sides of the demolition robot?

Rooted to the spot in his confusion, the Under-Leutna watched as the grenade began its journey back to its starting point. Suddenly understanding the implications, he turned to run for the trees, but it was too late. The light grenade landed at his feet and exploded in a scorching flash. The last thing to cross Mev's mind was an image of his daughter's face. He wondered just what Grand Leutna Shavan would do to her once she heard the news of his mission's failure. As the Under-Leutna fell to the ground, Rudy seemed to come to his senses. Bounding up the ramp, he turned to Lovell as he squeezed through the hatch.

'Do not fear failure, but rather fear not trying,' he said, although Lovell couldn't be sure if he heard Rudy's voice, or Sumara's.

'Looks like our timing was perfect,' grinned Zana from the controls. 'The Valiant has completed a full reboot. She's ready.'

'Take her up!' replied Lovell, keen to get under way.

'What about the zetron radiation?' Zana asked. 'You saw how it was destroying life on the island.'

'I gotta plan,' Lovell breathed. 'Trust me.'

Zana met his gaze. 'Always,' she smiled, and she leaned on the controls. A hum of engines filled the cockpit as the craft rose from the clearing.

'Wait,' said Vern from a monitor. 'These readings.' She tapped at the screen. 'Is this what brought you down on Yoba?'

'That's it,' Lovell nodded. 'Any ideas?'

'Stahn,' Vern called. 'Take a look at this.'

Her fellow scientist walked over from the medbed. Stahn had hooked Clarence up to a fluid drip that hung from the ceiling. Lovell noticed that the wound on his forearm was healing already.

Stahn nodded, his arms folded across his chest. 'Yup,' he said, 'that's our gravity well.'

Zana looked round as she lifted The Valiant's nose to the sky.

Vern sighed. 'We were ordered to hide the device until it was fully operational. That way, it could be moved into position without anyone noticing.' Her eyes flickered guiltily to the Kestran at the controls.

Lovell frowned. 'But how do you hide something the size of a small planetoid?'

'By bending space and time around it,' Stahn replied. 'Gravity wells had always been a theory.' There was a note of pride in his voice. 'We made them a reality.'

Vern took up the explanation. 'Space, light and even time itself is bent around it. It makes the Doomsday Device undetectable.'

'Unless you ran into it like we did,' Lovell scoffed.

Stahn frowned. 'That should never have happened. It was Tal's job to –' He broke off, as if the enormity of Tal's death had only just sunk in. Stahn blinked. 'It was Tal's job to phase shift the well so it couldn't be detected.'

Vern was looking thoughtful. 'He clearly failed, either by accident or design.' She met Stahn's gaze. 'He meant it to be discovered.' Vern turned to Colonel Zana. 'You have to believe us,' she pleaded, her eyes suddenly brimming with tears. 'Not all Zargons mean harm to your planet.'

Zana nodded. 'I know,' she said, softly.

'Wait,' Stahn said suddenly. 'You said you were en route somewhere when you encountered the well.' He looked Lovell in the eye. 'Where were you going?'

Lovell swallowed. 'We found evidence of what that weapon of yours can do.' He took a breath. 'We're heading to your home world to stop it.'

Stahn's eyes grew wild. Vern clutched at his arm for support. 'No,' she whispered. 'We can't go back there. They'll kill us.'

'We're *wanted* on the home world,' Stahn said, his voice unsteady.

Lovell puffed out his cheeks. 'Join the club,' he said. 'We need to find a way to disable that weapon. You said it's controlled from your home planet.' Stahn nodded. 'So that's where we start.' Lovell nodded to Colonel Zana. 'We just need to attend to a little unfinished business first.'

XIII
A PLAN IS HATCHED

The Valiant's tractor beam had lifted the stricken ambulance clear of the basin. As it lifted up beyond the clouds, it towed the vessel like a shmoolfish on a line.

'The island will recover in time,' Zana explained. 'It's a fitting resting place for your friends.'

Vern and Stahn nodded, their thoughts turning to their fallen comrades. 'Perhaps we'll return once all this is over,' whispered Vern, softly, 'and give them a proper burial.'

'That sounds like a good idea,' agreed Zana as she turned to the flight controls. 'I'm setting a course for the Zargon home world.' She looked meaningfully at the two scientists. 'Maybe you two can start figuring out how we disable that weapon.'

Stahn took a breath. 'I am sorry,' he said. 'And I am grateful.'

Zana blinked her wide, almond eyes. 'For what?'

'I am sorry for whatever the Zargons are planning to do to your people, and I am grateful for the risks you took to rescue us.'

Zana shook her head. 'Don't even mention it. Maybe you'll do the same for me one day.'

Vern smiled. 'That will be the day we can live in peace.' With a gentle nod to the Colonel, Vern led Stahn away to a bunk so they could begin to formulate a plan.

'No, really,' Clarence was protesting. 'I feel fine.'

'But Lovell says you must rest.' Jhy was pleading with the chimpanzee from beside the medbed. Though no longer hooked up to the drip, Clarence was still connected to various monitors via nodes attached to his body.

'But the medication has worked,' he insisted, gesturing to the screens around him. 'My stats are all perfectly normal. Besides, whoever listened to Lovell?'

Jhy turned as he heard a laugh behind him. Lovell smiled as he saw Clarence in good spirits again.

'Maybe you should start listening,' he grinned.

'Do you know something?' Clarence retorted, a mischievous twinkle in his eye. 'I have never, in all my life, found myself in any situation where I've thought to myself, *Clarence? You really should have listened to Lovell.*'

The two friends laughed as Lovell put a hand on Clarence's shoulder.

'Really,' Clarence assured him. 'I'm fine.'

'Okay,' Lovell agreed. 'All your readings are good, but I still want you to take it easy until we get to the Zargon home world. That zetron radiation really is no good for chimps.'

Clarence nodded. 'Like I said,' he grinned, 'I'm not your average chimpanzee.'

Their conversation was interrupted by Rudy stomping across the room, his heavy steps seeming to make the deck plates tremble. He held out his huge metal hands to show a newly repaired robot dog wagging his tail with excitement.

'You fixed him!' Jhy squeaked with delight, reaching out to scoop Dash into his arms. 'Thanks, Rudy!'

Rudy seemed almost abashed. 'It was nothing,' he rumbled.

'No, really,' Lovell interjected. 'It was only a few months ago that you couldn't build a stack of cups without crushing them. Now, you're performing precision welding.'

Rudy shrugged his heavy shoulders. 'I have a good teacher,' he said. Lovell frowned as the demolition robot made his way back to the workbench. By now, Clarence had detached himself from his medbed. Swinging his legs to the floor, he grabbed Jhy by the hand and led him towards the flight deck, eager to monitor their progress.

'Did Rudy just say he *has* a good teacher?' came Zana's voice from the door as Clarence and Jhy passed her. 'Present tense? Does he mean Sumara?'

Lovell sighed and scratched the stubble on his chin. 'I think,' he began, conscious of how ridiculous he was about to sound, 'that he has something of Sumara inside him.'

Zana raised her eyebrows as she looked over at the demolition robot. Rudy was methodically tidying away his tools. 'How so?'

'I dunno,' admitted Lovell, 'but Rudy was with him when he died. Is it possible that Sumara's spirit has been transferred into Rudy's circuits? Jhy called it his *shulka.*'

Zana shook her head in wonder. 'Nothing would surprise me about that man,' she smiled. 'And you saw what Rudy did with that light grenade? That was pure Sumara.'

'It's weird,' grumbled Lovell.

'No,' Zana admonished him. 'It's wonderful.'

'Colonel Zana?' came Stahn's voice by the door. Vern stood next to him, an expression of determination on her face. 'We think we know how to destroy the Doomsday Device.'

The two scientists sat around the table with Lovell, Zana, Clarence and Jhy. Rudy stood some way off, his eyes glowing in concentration. Truth be told, Lovell found his presence rather disconcerting. Was it Rudy who was looking at him, or Sumara? Lovell shuddered.

'May I?' asked Stahn, indicating the controls on the tabletop.

'Be my guest,' Colonel Zana smiled.

Stahn stabbed at the buttons. Lovell found himself staring at a three dimensional image of a planet, hovering a few inches above the table's surface.

'The Zargon home world?' he asked.

Stahn nodded. 'We've hacked into their monitoring systems. This is a detailed survey of the entire planet's surface and all buildings belonging to the Elite.'

'Wait,' interjected Colonel Zana. 'You hacked into their systems from this ship? How the hell did you manage that?'

Vern smiled. 'Well, it certainly helps that I designed them,' she winked. 'And it seems they haven't yet thought to change the access codes.'

'What's the Elite?' Lovell asked.

'The Zargon ruling caste,' Stahn explained. 'Militaristic, privileged and powerful. They set policy and rule the planet through military might.'

'They've ruled for centuries,' Vern added. 'Dissent is not tolerated.'

Zana was enthralled. 'Which makes your actions all the more courageous,' she said.

Stahn took a breath. 'Which brings us to how we destroy the device.' He flicked a switch and the image changed. The space-bound weapon hung before them, its menacing claws curled beneath it like a predator biding its time, waiting to strike.

The scientist broke the silence. 'It's just about impregnable,' Stahn began, 'but there is one weakness.' He toggled a switch and the picture zoomed in on a section of the device's upper hull. 'The plasma cannon operates at massively high temperatures, so it needs cooling.'

Vern pointed towards a series of open hatches on the surface. 'These vents suck superheated coolant from the cannon and release it into space as a gas.'

'So that's our way in?' Lovell asked.

'They're too small for any of us,' Stahn replied. He toggled another switch and the image changed again. This time, a red line showed the routes taken for the gas to escape through the vents. 'The original duct is huge,' Stahn explained, 'but then it diverges into dozens of smaller ones, about five kilometres from the surface.'

'The idea,' added Vern, 'was to avoid the prospect of a large exhaust port. It would be too vulnerable to attack.'

'Which is why the external vents are tiny. Barely big enough to fit an arm through.' Stahn was pointing to where the red line divided. 'Block that junction, just where the duct divides into the smaller vents and, once the plasma coils are engaged, they would overheat.'

Vern nodded. 'Ka-boom.'

'Okay,' said Clarence, 'so how do we get in there if none of us would fit?'

'One of us would fit,' Jhy retorted.

'Sorry, kid,' said Lovell gently. 'Looks like even you'd be too big.'

'I wasn't thinking of me.' Jhy lowered his gaze to the robot dog nestled in his lap. 'Dash would fit.'

Lovell looked to the two scientists for confirmation.

'He looks small enough,' Vern confirmed.

'Okay, then what?' Zana frowned. 'Say we get him to the junction, what then? Would he be enough to stop the gas escaping?'

'Like a cork in a bottle!' Lovell regretted the analogy immediately.

'He'd be destroyed in the heat,' Stahn replied. 'He'd need to collapse the duct. It's built of heat resistant material but it's susceptible to photon bombardment. That would be enough to hold the gas and cause a chain reaction. Then he – and you – would have to get out quick.'

'But Dash doesn't have a photonic weapon,' Jhy pointed out.

Colonel Zana was thinking hard. 'I think we have all the parts we need on The Valiant. We just need someone to fit them.'

Rudy stood suddenly to attention. 'I stand ready,' he growled.

'Yes,' exclaimed Jhy. 'Rudy can do it!'

Lovell nodded. Somehow, he felt proud of the robot Rudy had become. It was hard to believe that, when they had first met, the demolition robot with the glowing eyes could barely even walk into a room without causing chaos.

'Okay,' said Lovell as he turned back to the scientists, 'I guess this is when you tell us the hard part.'

Vern leaned over to flick a switch, and the picture flipped back to the Zargon home world.

'The problem,' she said, 'is the gravity well.'

Lovell sighed. 'I thought it might be.'

'Obviously, you can't get near the device while the well is active.'

'Tell us about it,' sneered Clarence.

'So, we have to deactivate it.'

Lovell leaned on his elbows, keen to hear more. 'You said you'd hacked into the Zargon systems. Can you deactivate it from here?'

Vern shook her head. 'Unfortunately not.' She reached her hand towards the image and spread her fingers wide. As she did so, the picture zoomed in on a multi-storey construction in the heart of a city. 'This is mission control.' A room in the basement of the building flashed red. 'We'll need access to the control room. Inside is a console housing the gravity well controls. To deactivate it, two keys need to be turned at the exact same moment by two different operatives.'

Lovell looked hopeful. 'Tell me you have those keys.'

With a look to each other, the two scientists reached beneath their uniforms to retrieve two keys, each fastened to a chain around their necks.

'You're sure they'll work?' Zana asked.

Vern shrugged. 'I don't see why not. As far as they're concerned we left the home world, never to return. They'd have no reason to change the keys.'

Stahn indicated the display. 'They haven't even changed the access codes to their systems.'

'So, where's the *but*?' asked Lovell.

Clarence caught his eye and smiled. 'There's *always* a but.'

Stahn sighed. 'The *but* is, once the gravity well is deactivated, we'll have to engage the plasma coils, and everyone will know about it. And they'll try and stop it.'

Lovell leaned back on his chair. 'So, we land on the home world and get you into that control room without being detected. In the meantime, The Valiant flies to this weapon and waits for the gravity well to be deactivated. Once its switched off, The Valiant lands and drops Dash down a vent shaft to collapse the duct, while the whole of the Zargon Empire is chasing us down, having been alerted to our presence by the deactivation of the gravity well.'

Stahn nodded. 'Sounds about right.'

'It's impossible, isn't it?' asked Vern, suddenly downcast.

'Maybe,' chirped Clarence. 'But *impossible* is our specialty.'

Zana stood up. 'Okay,' she began. 'Clarence and Rudy will get you into that control room. Lovell's a wanted man and I... Well, let's just say I don't think a Kestran would be too welcome on the Zargon home world right now. So Lovell, Jhy, Dash and I will take The Valiant back to that device and wait for it to appear.' Everyone round the table nodded in understanding. Zana turned to the two scientists. 'Don't worry,' she said, 'we'll give you weapons.'

'How do we get close to the home world in this ship without them detecting us?' Vern asked, not unreasonably.

Lovell grinned. 'We don't need to. Remember, we're towing your ambulance.'

'But the zetron radiation,' Stahn began.

'There's your reason for landing,' Lovell shrugged. 'Emergency repairs. They'll think nothing of it. We'll drop you in orbit, then head back out to the device.'

'See?' Clarence winked to Vern. 'We laugh in the face of *impossible*.'

XIV
FOOL'S GOLD

R o Silvari didn't think much of the Zargon home world. The air seemed to sting her lungs and leave an acrid taste in her mouth. Even as she was marched through the antiseptic corridors of the military headquarters, she was sure she could see an unhealthy haze hanging in the air.

Ro had been waiting for this moment. Now that John Lovell had been dealt with, she was eager for her reward. Having played her part so well, she was sure the Zargons would approve the transfer of Lovell's gold. She had hidden herself away for weeks, waiting for her paymasters to contact her. At last, having heard nothing but a deafening silence, she had taken matters into her own hands. She had rented a small, dilapidated planet hopper. It was barely space worthy. As she had approached the Zargon home world, she had contacted the Elite to let them know she was on her way. As expected, they had provided quite the welcoming committee. No fewer than six stormtroopers had been dispatched to accompany her from the spaceport, all of them armed with Heat Exchange Guns. Ro had thought nothing of it. The Zargons were notorious for being jumpy.

As she was led from an elevator onto one of the higher floors of the building, Ro began to think about how her life was about to change. One million credits in gold bars would sure come in useful. It was enough to buy a hideaway on a tropical rim world, or a ranch on the smaller of the frontier planets. For the first time in her life, Ro Silvari would be in possession of that rarest of commodities; choice. The universe seemed to open up before her.

A door hissed o one side, and Ro was led into a room lined with glass. The huge windows looked down on the city beneath. Or, at least, they would have done had the smog not got in the way. Even from this great height, Ro could see the noxious clouds churning below, raining poison onto the open streets.

In the furthest corner stood a woman, silhouetted by the dim light beyond. Just as Ro began to wonder if she would ever move, the woman raised a hand to dismiss the guards. Ro stood in silence.

Turning at last, Grand Leutna Shavan surveyed her guest. 'You look older in real life,' she sneered.

Ro was taken aback until she remembered Lovell's trial had been broadcast. And, of course, the Grand Leutna would have been very interested in the outcome.

'Being poor does that to a woman,' Ro shot back. 'Which is why I've come for my payment.'

'Lovell's gold?' Shavan looked back out the window to the clouds beyond.

'*My* gold,' Ro corrected her. There was another silence. 'So, if you'll just –'

'Lovell is free,' Shavan said suddenly.

Ro was confused. 'No,' she began, carefully. 'Lovell is at the Nebula Penitentiary. If he isn't, he'll be dead.'

With an enigmatic look, Shavan walked to a smoked glass table inlaid with copper circuitry. As she waved her hand over the tabletop, an image of a man appeared, gaunt looking and dressed in a three-piece suit.

'This is Governor Dravit from The Nebula Penitentiary,' Shavan explained with mock patience. 'I received this message just this morning.'

With another wave of her hand, the image began to move. 'I regret to inform you,' Dravit began, 'that Prisoner 403 has absconded.' He swallowed. Ro thought he looked nervous. 'Rest assured, ma'am, I have no doubt he will be captured and returned to the Penitentiary in the near future. In the meantime, I have launched a full review of our security procedures.' The image disappeared in a blast of static.

'Prisoner 403?' Ro blinked.

Shavan's reply was slow and deliberate. 'John... D... Lovell.'

'But that can't be possible,' Ro stammered. 'And if he *has* escaped, how is that my fault?'

'Oh, don't worry,' Shavan purred. 'I'm not blaming you.' She smiled an unnerving smile. 'No, Governor Dravit is solely to blame for Lovell's escape. Or should I say, *ex* Governor Dravit.' She reached down to press a button on the table. 'Let me know when the execution has been completed,' she hissed into the comms panel.

'Yes, Grand Leutna,' came the reply.

Satisfied at the response, Shavan moved closer to her guest until the two women stood almost toe-to-toe. 'As you know,' Shavan said, softly, 'we had a deal. Lovell's death, for Lovell's gold.'

Ro shook her head. She had a feeling she knew where this conversation was headed. 'I fulfilled my part of the bargain.'

'But, Lovell lives,' Shavan said. 'That is a statement of fact.' The Grand Leutna turned back to the window. 'And if Lovell lives, he's a threat to our latest operation. There is, of course, a way to redeem yourself.'

Ro noticed Shavan's fingers flexing behind her back. 'Name it.'

'Find him, kill him, and you'll get your gold.'

Ro was taken aback. 'Why me?' She was sure she heard Shavan laughing in response.

'Because you have the greatest motivation of all,' the Grand Leutna chuckled. 'Greater than duty, greater even than fear.' She turned again to fix Ro in her gaze. 'Greed,' she grimaced. 'There are a million reasons why you'll kill John Lovell, and they're currently stacked in a pile inside a secure safe at the Zargon Military Bank.'

Ro bit her lip. 'I'll find him,' she said at last. 'And I'll be back for payment.'

Their conversation at an end, the guards were summoned to escort Ro Silvari from the room and back to the spaceport. As the door hissed shut behind her, a soft repetitive beeping filled the room.

'Yes?' Shavan snapped, her finger on the comms button.

'Grand Leutna,' came a nervous voice from the speaker. 'I have news of Under-Leutna Mev and his mission to Yoba.'

Shavan grit her teeth. She could already tell from the tremor in his voice that, whatever he had to say, it was far from the news she wanted to hear.

XV
THE LION'S DEN

The Valiant had been equipped with the latest anti-detection technology. Together with Stahn having access to the Zargons' security systems, it meant that the sleek Kestran ship slipped into the Zargon home world's orbit completely unnoticed.

'That's it,' Colonel Zana announced from the flight console. 'We're safe enough from their scans here, but we get any closer and they'll see us for sure.'

Clarence whistled from the co-pilot's chair. 'I'm picking up lots of pollution in the atmosphere. Carbon monoxide, nitrogen and sulphur dioxide, all in high concentrations.'

'Welcome to my planet,' whispered Vern.

'What happened?' asked Zana.

'Industrialisation, massive and quick, and all for the sake of the military.' Vern squinted through the windshield. 'Every unit of power we produce is funnelled to the Elite for their military machine, while the population starve and grow sick on pollutants.'

'Our planet is dying,' Stahn added. 'The natural ecosystems have broken down, meaning nothing can grow. No plants, no crops.'

Zana sensed that such thoughts could not be so freely expressed on the planet below. 'But Kestra has all the power it needs from its libidium core.' She took a breath before continuing. 'And the Zargons want it for themselves. That's what the Doomsday Device is for.'

Stahn nodded. 'I fear you're right. With a libidium power source, the Elite could become more powerful.'

'No matter what the cost to Kestra.' Zana's almond eyes were moist with tears.

Lovell turned to the scientists, determined to lift the mood. 'Okay guys, time to suit up. This is as far as we take you.'

With the small crew safely on board the ambulance, Clarence gave the okay for The Valiant to release its tractor beam. As he watched the craft slip gracefully away into the darkness of space, the chimpanzee strapped himself into the ambulance's pilot seat.

'Just like it was made for me,' he said, oblivious to the fact that his hairy feet barely reached the floor. He flicked some switches on the dashboard. 'We've just got enough power to get us down safely,' he announced, peering at the monitors. 'And it looks like we're already transmitting an autodocking code.'

Stahn nodded. 'It's an emergency vehicle. I guess it saves time.'

'Hmm,' Clarence replied. 'That makes things a little easier.'

Behind them, Rudy was inspecting the weapons Colonel Zana had given them from The Valiant's armoury.

'These are powerful,' he rumbled. 'But not as powerful as Rudy.'

Vern strapped herself in beside the giant robot, readying herself for the descent through the atmosphere.

'I've never fired a gun before,' she admitted.

Rudy slammed a pulse rifle into her chest. 'Point,' he growled. 'Shoot.'

Clarence couldn't help but laugh. 'That's about as concise a lesson as I've ever heard.' He leaned on the controls and angled the ship's nose down to the planet's surface. 'Okay,' he cautioned, 'this is where it gets bumpy.' He reached up to toggle a switch. Somewhere, a siren blared. Lights flashed through the windshield. Clarence's face broke into a broad, simian grin. 'I've always wanted to do that.'

The ambulance screamed through the upper atmosphere. In just a few minutes, toxic rain was lashing at the windshield. Clarence gripped the controls as he felt the craft buffeted by wind. Vern looked to Stahn.

'I never thought we'd be back,' she whispered. Stahn nodded, sadly, and squeezed her hand.

There was a buzz of static from the comms. 'Emergency vehicle,' came a clipped voice. 'You are cleared to dock at tower three. We are adjusting your docking code.' Clarence noticed lights blinking on the control panel. 'We have detected damage to your vehicle,' the voice continued. 'Do you require assistance?'

Clarence looked to the scientists for guidance. Vern nodded that he should press the comms to reply.

'Er, no,' she called as Clarence held down the button. 'No, thank you. We can effect the repairs ourselves.'

There was a silence. 'He's consulting with his superiors,' Stahn whispered.

'Very well,' came the voice at last. 'We'll send you a maintenance robot. Tower three.' The comms clicked off. The cabin gave a sudden jolt as the autodocking procedures kicked in and Clarence sat back, his hands behind his head. 'My kind of flying,' he smiled.

Soon, the docking tower loomed large through the windshield. It was one of four similar structures, bristling with docking arms and antennae. Clarence could see ships of various sizes arriving and departing. 'Busy place,' he mused. 'How far to the control room?'

Now the ride was smoother, Stahn unclipped his restraints and joined the chimp at the dashboard. 'These towers are pretty central,' he explained, pointing through the glass. 'We'll take that conduit to the central plaza, then it's a matter of gaining entry to the Military Headquarters.'

Clarence nodded. 'I guess we're not going to walk through the front door?'

Stahn nodded back to the large demolition robot in the cabin. 'Not with him at our disposal.'

The ambulance changed course. Clarence could see a vacant docking port ahead. 'Okay,' he breathed. 'Looks like we're going in.'

Stahn took his seat again and picked up his pulse rifle. It felt cold and unyielding in his grip, and he shuddered at the thought he might actually have to fire it.

Clarence felt the ambulance's docking clamps extend from the hull and the controls before him seemed to shift subtly of their own accord. The vehicle slowed as it made its approach until it was inching imperceptibly towards the tower. Finally, it made contact with a jolt and a hiss of air. The docking clamps were engaged.

The chimpanzee leaned forward to flick a switch. The cockpit monitors showed the view directly outside the ambulance. A small concourse was busy with people and robots.

'Okay,' sighed Stahn, nervously, 'now all we gotta do is figure out how we get out of here unnoticed with a talking chimp and a giant robot.'

Clarence was peering at the screen as a small maintenance robot trundled round the corner. 'I think I may have the answer,' he grinned.

The door slid open with a hiss of hydraulics. The repair robot waited patiently for the ramp to descend. It was an old model, battered and scratched. Over the years, it had operated on rim worlds and asteroid colonies. It had fixed everything from great space liners to mining ships. Now, it was destined to end its days in the service of the Zargon Empire. In appearance, it resembled nothing more than a box on legs. A squat dome of a head swivelled this way and that as it made a cursory assessment of the damage. The robot readied its four extendable arms as it waited for the boarding ramp to extend, attaching the tools it thought most appropriate to the task. At last, it trundled up the ramp and through the door, only to be confronted by the biggest robot it had ever seen. As Vern punched at the door controls to retract the ramp and close the hatch, Rudy grabbed the robot's head in his vice-like hands.

'Sorry,' he growled as, with a shower of sparks, it came clean away from the robot's body.

When the ambulance door opened again, it was to let out two scientists, a huge robot and a squat, box-like maintenance robot. They made their way down the ramp onto the crowded concourse, headed for the entrance to the conduit corridor.

'You okay in there?' Vern whispered.

The repair robot's head swivelled in response. 'It's a bit snug,' Clarence admitted from inside. 'Like wearing someone else's suit.'

As the little party turned towards the exit, they were approached by two Zargon guards. Even inside his metal casing, Clarence could feel his two scientist companions tensing in anticipation.

'What's that?' asked the taller of the guards, gesturing to Rudy with the point of his gun.

Vern swallowed. 'Demolition robot. We're taking it for repurposing.'

'For military use,' Stahn added stiffly. He could feel the cold metal of his pulse rifle pressing against his ribs. He and Vern had strapped their weapons beneath their uniforms before they left the ambulance.

The shorter soldier nodded over to the landing pad. 'That your vehicle?'

Stahn nodded.

'Why is the Science Corps in possession of an ambulance?'

Vern was sure she noticed his finger squeezing on the trigger of his gun. She thought fast. 'Budget cuts,' she sighed. 'I mean, we were hoping for a fully kitted out science vessel, but that's all we were given.' She nudged Stahn.

'Oh, yeah,' he spluttered. 'I think it's been decommissioned. At least, that's what they told us. Seems that, if your work has no military use, you're stuffed. So, we had to use that.'

'What are you working on?' demanded the first soldier.

'We've been out on the rim worlds,' bluffed Vern. 'Looking at various quarrying techniques.' She looked at Rudy. 'That's where we found this guy. We thought he'd come in useful.'

Even through their helmets, Vern could tell the soldiers were losing interest. 'That repair robot,' the taller man said. 'Have it sent to the air farms when you're done with it. They got a problem with the purifiers.'

Vern gave a curt nod as they moved off. 'Will do.'

'Quarrying techniques?' asked Stahn from the corner of his mouth.

'It was my final semester project at the Academy,' Vern smiled. 'It's as dull as it sounds.'

The crowd was thinning as they walked. Aside from the occasional glance at Rudy, they were attracting very little interest. At last they came to an open square lined with buildings that soared into the sky. Here, in the open, the air was thick with pollutants. Through a grill in the maintenance robot's head, Clarence could see the poorest of the home world's citizens sheltering from the stinging rain. Much of the square was home to a shantytown made of wooden pallets and blankets. Even in his cramped condition, the chimp could sense an atmosphere of desperation and menace.

'That building is the Military Headquarters,' Stahn explained. 'The control room is right beneath our feet.'

'Why underground?' asked Clarence.

'The building is home to many divisions of the military,' Vern replied. 'Science Corps at the bottom, the Elite at the top.'

'The higher up you go,' Stahn sighed, 'the more important you are.'

'But, you said your control room is in the basement.' Clarence was bemused.

Stahn shrugged. 'Just goes to show what they think of scientists. We're tolerated, so long as the science agrees with them.'

'We usually use that entrance there.' Vern nodded to a large atrium leading to the forbidding looking tower block. It was patrolled by armed soldiers from the Elite Guard and barricaded by large concrete blocks. Security cameras were hung from every corner. Clarence could just about make out a few visitors waiting in line for the walk-through scanners. It looked impregnable.

'Please tell me you've got another plan,' whispered Clarence.

'Of course we do,' Stahn smiled. 'He's standing right beside you.' The scientist moved nearer to Rudy. 'We're heading for the south east corner of the plaza. I'll let you know when we're in the right spot.'

Rudy nodded his great head. With a whirring of gears, he followed the little group to a secluded corner of the square. The makeshift tents and hovels were fewer in number here. As Stahn looked around, it was clear to see why. An acrid liquid was dripping from a nearby pipe and collecting in a large, foul smelling pool. He didn't want to know what it was. 'This is it, Rudy,' he whispered, blinking against the sting of the air. As the robot prepared himself for action, the scientist reached inside the folds of his uniform. 'This is where things are going to get a little heated,' he said to Vern, pulling his pulse rifle from its holster.

Vern nodded, bending to lift her trouser leg. Untying the straps that held her rifle to her calf, she straightened up and unlocked the safety clip.

'Whatever resistance we get,' she hissed to Clarence, 'we'll hold them off as long as possible. You'll need to get us into that control room. The door was always opened by a guard, so we never had the code. You'll need to crack the lock to get us in.'

'Gotcha,' came Clarence's voice from the maintenance robot.

'Okay, Rudy,' Stahn nodded with a final look around. 'Let's do it.'

XVI
FRIEND OR FOE

Its ion engines blazing, The Valiant slipped silently through space. Colonel Zana peered through the cockpit windshield. The stars were a blur.

'We're coming up on the coordinates,' Lovell announced. There was no response. Unclipping his restraints, he leaned on the dashboard and waved a hand in front of Zana's face. 'Penny for your thoughts?' he teased.

Zana seemed to snap to life. 'Uh, sorry,' she mumbled, reaching out to disengage the ion drive. The familiar rumble of the impulse engines returned.

'You okay?' Lovell asked, concerned.

Zana thought for a moment, then turned to meet Lovell's gaze. 'How can they hate us so much,' she asked, simply, 'to expend so much time, energy and resources on building a thing to destroy us?'

Lovell sighed and slumped back into his seat. 'When I was a kid,' he said, 'I lived on a ranch with my dad, miles from nowhere. Life was tough and we didn't have much. Our nearest neighbour lived on the other side of the valley. I could just see the lights of their house from my bed at night.' The old captain had a wistful look in his eye. 'There was a kid that lived there. He had less than we had.' He could see Zana was wondering where this was headed. 'Anyways,' Lovell continued, 'one day my dad gave me an old seed robot he'd won in a bet. Nothin' special. It had one eye, its compressor servos were half hanging out, you know the kinda thing. It barely worked at all, but I loved it.' Lovell smiled at the memory. 'I made a leash out of old leather and took it for walks. We went everywhere together. And the boy across the valley saw me. Once, I caught him in a tree, watching as I played with the old seed robot. Next day, it was gone.'

Zana raised an eyebrow. 'Gone?'

'Yup,' Lovell nodded, 'and I was pretty sure where.'

'What did you do?' Zana leaned forward on her chair.

'I went to confront him. Hiked right across the valley on the hottest day of the year.'

Zana was enthralled.

'When I got there, I saw he had even less than I did. His family looked poor. Their ranch was... pitiful. The buildings were falling apart and they clearly didn't have the time or the money to fix them up. I started to feel sorry for him.' Lovell stretched his arms above his head. 'So, I found him in a barn. He was sitting in the light from a broken window. And there on the floor, I saw my old seed robot, taken apart, its pieces just lying on the floor around him.'

'Why?' Zana asked.

'My question, exactly,' Lovell nodded. 'I was crying. I wanted to know why he'd done it. D'you know what he said?'

Zana shook her head.

Lovell leaned forward. '*I wanted to see why it made you happy.*'

There was a silence.

'Wait.' Zana looked confused. 'Is there a lesson in there somewhere?'

Lovell puffed out his cheeks. 'I guess some people always want what someone else has got.'

Zana rolled her eyes. 'Well,' she sighed, 'thanks for the insight.' She reached out to the flight controls. 'I'm bringing us to a dead stop. Now, we wait for Rudy and Clarence to work their magic.'

'Lovell?' Jhy had walked into the cockpit, his pet dog wagging its tail excitedly beside him. 'Dash says he's ready. He has calibrated his new weapons. He's really quite good with them.'

'That's great,' Lovell enthused. 'Remember, he just needs to close that duct. Nothing fancy. A few blasts should do it, then get the hell outta there.'

'Did you know, Jhy,' Zana asked suddenly, 'that Lovell had a pet robot as a kid?'

Lovell almost choked. 'Well, I wouldn't say it was a pet, exactly.'

Jhy looked aghast. 'Really?'

'And he loved it *so* much,' Zana teased.

'Aww, Lovell,' Jhy snuggled into Lovell's stomach, wrapping his arms around him in a forceful hug. 'I didn't know we had so much in common!'

Lovell's evident discomfort was interrupted by a sudden bang on the ship's hull. 'What the hell?'

Zana spun quickly to the controls. 'There's a ship directly above us. A small hopper. Looks like it's trying to dock.'

'How could you miss that?' Lovell moved Jhy gently to one side.

Zana was suddenly defensive. 'Because I was too wrapped up in stories of someone's childhood.' A warning beep sounded from the dashboard. 'Wait,' she said, a puzzled look on her face. 'They're not coming in through the hatch, they're coming in through the –'

A flash of light filled the cockpit as a shower of sparks fell from above their heads.

'Ceiling,' Zana concluded, redundantly. A jagged section of The Valiant's roof fell to the floor with a clang. Lovell peered through the smoke as a tall figure in combat fatigues dropped through the hole. Lovell gasped as it removed its helmet.

'Colonel Zana?' Lovell rose from his chair, his thumbs in his belt loops. 'May I introduce Ro Silvari?'

Before Zana could move, Ro had reached for the blaster buckled to her belt. 'You can sit down with the kid, lady,' Ro drawled. 'It's Lovell I want.'

'You and just about every other woman in the galaxy,' Lovell winked.

Ro let go a sigh. 'I see your time in The Neb did nothing to improve your sense of humour.'

Lovell clenched his fists. 'Yeah, about that. Why did you frame me for Threep's death? You know I had nothing to do with it.'

'Of course I know that,' Ro sneered. 'You wouldn't have it in you. Threep would've sent you away with your head up your –'

'Hey!' Jhy interrupted, puffing out his chest. 'What do you want with my friend?'

Ro laughed. 'Your *friend* here is worth a lot to me, kid.' She looked at Lovell, pointedly. 'About one million credits.'

'That's my gold,' Lovell protested.

'Yeah, but I figure you owe me.' Ro swung herself onto Lovell's empty seat. 'Nice ship by the way,' she smiled at Zana.

'How did you find us?' The Colonel was in no mood for pleasantries. 'The Valiant has got state of the art defences.'

Ro laughed to herself. 'I found you the old fashioned way,' she chuckled. 'A little bit of luck, and a little bit of this.' She tapped her temple. 'Turns out you were leaving Zargon orbit just as I was leaving, too.'

'You were on the home world?' Lovell shook his head in disbelief. 'Why?'

'To collect my reward,' Ro hissed. 'Like *that* was ever gonna happen. I should've known you'd scupper it. Why can't you ever stay in one place long enough, John Lovell?' Ro reached inside a breast pocket to pull out a half chewed spanga root. She pulled at the dry ends with her fingers before jamming it between her teeth. 'Don't get too used to him, honey,' she said with a look to Zana. 'He won't stick around.'

Zana blinked. 'Oh, we're not – ' she began.

'But how did you follow us?' Lovell asked, pointing at the ship's monitors. 'That little hopper is no match for The Valiant.'

Ro grinned, mischievously. 'You'd think, wouldn't you? Firstly, I wondered why a ship like this would be in orbit around the Zargon home world. It's like nothing I've ever seen before. It's definitely not Zargon. And so I followed you out of orbit. Then I saw you fire up those ion engines and I decided to ride the slipstream.'

'You tailgated an ion ship?' Lovell's eyes were wide. 'You're crazy.'

Ro shrugged, nonplussed. 'So they say. But then you dropped out of warp right here. Right near the gravity well.'

Zana narrowed her almond eyes. 'How do you know about that?'

'Oh, I don't know what it's for, or what it's hiding,' Ro clarified, 'but I know *where* it is and I know that it's dangerous. I ran into it myself a couple of weeks back. Then, I thought, who do I know that's stupid enough to run *toward* danger?' She gestured to Lovell. '*Voila*.' She looked the old captain in the eye. 'So, how did you get off The Neb?'

'I escaped,' Lovell said, triumphantly. 'With a little help from my friends.'

Ro leaned back and lifted her feet onto the dashboard. 'Well, obviously you escaped,' she scoffed. 'That was my plan all along. But you escaped too soon. Now I have to kill you.'

'What do you mean *your* plan?' Zana was fighting the impulse to knock the woman's feet off her flight controls.

'Listen lady, I don't know how things are on Kestra, but in the rest of the universe, there's only one thing gets you where you wanna go. Money. The one thing I've never had.'

'Threep looked after you,' Lovell countered.

'Oh sure, Threep did his best.' Ro turned away. Lovell was sure it was so he wouldn't see the tears welling in her eyes. 'But it's been years now. What's a woman to do?'

'Hustle, like the rest of us,' Lovell replied. 'Not sell your friends out for gold.'

Ro was suddenly defiant. 'Here's something you don't know about Threep Silvari,' she hissed, her eyes burning. 'Wonderful old Threep, everybody's friend, never one to turn his back on those in need. He died in debt.' Ro wiped her eyes with the back of her hand. 'He owed just about everyone in the galaxy and the day he died, they all came looking for payback.'

Lovell was astonished. 'Threep? In debt?' It made no sense. 'But I thought he'd made his fortune in exports.'

Ro nodded. 'Made it and lost it,' she sighed. 'And when those that he owed came looking, they found me. And I was broke. I've been on the run ever since, with just that hopper to my name.'

'But it was mean to send Lovell to jail!' Jhy exclaimed. Colonel Zana reached out to touch him lightly by the arm.

Lovell nodded. 'I mean, he's got a point.'

'Maybe,' Ro shrugged. 'But did you ever stop to think why it was so easy to do?'

Lovell looked hurt. 'I never knew you hated me so much.'

'It's not about that.' Ro Silvari laughed again. 'It was easy to do because I knew you'd be okay.' She gave Lovell a knowing smile. 'And it looks like I was right.'

Lovell was struggling to contain his rage. 'I was sent to The Nebula Penitentiary!'

'And you escaped, as you so proudly told me a moment ago. And as I knew you would. The great John D Lovell is gonna die in a blaze of glory, not executed without ceremony in some far off prison.'

Lovell clenched his fists. 'If there weren't children in the room…' he hissed, half an eye on Jhy.

'Don't think you're getting off this ship with him,' Zana warned.

Ro laughed again. 'They are desperate to see you dead, Lovell. What did you do to them?'

'He saved Kestra,' cried Jhy, 'and he's about to do it again.'

Ro nodded. 'Oh yeah, I heard about your adventure on the Zargon asteroid. You and your little team.'

'He's proven himself to us again and again,' said Zana, leaping to Lovell's defence. 'The galaxy can't do without him.'

'Oh?' Ro was suddenly interested. 'Sounds serious. What's up?'

'That gravity well,' Lovell began. 'It's hiding something terrible. A weapon so powerful it'll tear Kestra apart.'

'How?'

'It's going to extract our planet's core,' Zana continued. 'The Zargons are desperate for a new energy source, so they're going to use ours.'

'Huh?' Ro was perplexed. 'What power source?'

'Kestra's core is pure libidium, a highly reactive element but clean and safe.'

'We're going to stop them,' added Lovell.

There was a pause as Ro Silvari weighed up the situation. If she was careful, it could be to her advantage.

'So, he's an essential part of the team, huh?' she said with a look to Zana.

'Invaluable is the word,' the colonel agreed.

'And *valuable*, too.'

'Sure.' Zana had a feeling she knew where this was headed.

'So, let's say I didn't take him back to the home world, that I didn't collect my gold.'

'*My* gold,' rasped Lovell, indignant.

Zana smiled. 'There's plenty more where that came from. And I have a direct line to the Kestran President.'

'Is that so?' Ro thought for a moment then slowly, and very deliberately, she placed her blaster on the dashboard. 'Shall we say two million credits?'

Zana shook her head. 'A million.'

'Wait,' Lovell protested. 'Are you haggling over me?'

'A woman's gotta live.' Ro folded her arms. 'I can get a million from the Zargons in exchange for his body. A million and a half and we're done.'

Zana looked serious. 'A million and a half, then. You have my word.'

XVII

DOWN BELOW

Rudy pummelled his fists into the ground. Stahn was amazed at how little attention he drew to himself. Despite the noise of the giant robot's hands slicing into the ground, barely a single person turned to look. No doubt, the scientist thought, they were too concerned with scratching a living among the tents and shacks. Perhaps they had simply learned not to interfere in matters that did not concern them.

Rudy's arms were a blur. First, the pavement slabs were smashed and torn aside. Then, the ground beneath was scooped away into a great bank of debris. Soon the trench was metres deep, with Rudy standing amongst the dirt like a child at the beach. At last, his fist broke through to the structure underneath. A great hole opened up and the earth fell through to the corridor below.

'He's through!' Vern gasped, holding her gun at the ready.

'I'm gonna be more use out of this thing now,' announced Clarence. Unscrewing the maintenance robot's head from the inside, he let it drop to the ground with a clang and heaved himself from the robot's metal casing. 'There are certainly better ways to travel,' he grinned.

As Rudy dropped through the hole to the corridor beneath, Stahn could already hear signs of commotion. He cocked his gun and gestured that Vern and Clarence should do the same. 'Ready?'

'As I'll ever be,' Vern nodded, a look of determination on her face.

With a final glance to his fellow raiders, Stahn jumped into the pit.

Rudy was crouching directly beneath the hole in the ceiling, his great bulk acting as both a defence against the advancing Zargon guards and as a way down to the floor for his companions. Stahn found what toe holds he could, clambering from the robot's shoulders to his knees to the ground. All around him, he could hear the familiar sound of ice bullets ricocheting off the walls and Rudy's metal armour. The huge robot was proving to be an effective barricade. Dropping to one knee, Stahn took aim at the advancing guards. A blast of laser fire saw two of them drop to the floor, their guns falling silent.

'Why haven't the alarms gone off?' asked Clarence as he dropped to the scientist's side.

'Only the doors and entrances are alarmed,' yelled Stahn above the noise. 'They never expected anyone to get in through the roof!' Letting go a volley of laser fire, Stahn pointed behind them. 'That's the door to the control room,' he shouted. 'You'll need to crack the code to get us in.'

As Vern lowered herself from Rudy's chest to take his place, Clarence scampered to the door.

'How you holding up, Rudy?' Vern yelled as she fired around his great bulk.

'Barely a scratch,' he rumbled.

Ahead of them, Stahn noticed one of the guards had unclipped a light grenade from his belt. 'Rudy!' the scientist yelled. 'Incoming!'

As the grenade arced its way down the corridor Rudy readied himself for action. With one perfectly timed swing of his arm, he sent the projectile hurtling back towards the Zargon guards. The effect was immediate. With a sudden panic, the guards scrambled back up the corridor, trying to put as much distance between themselves and the impending explosion as they could. Two of them fell to the floor in the commotion, only to find themselves trampled beneath the boots of their retreating comrades.

The flash, when it came, was blinding. As Vern and Stahn shielded their eyes, the corridor was lit by a bright, searing light. Rudy stood his ground against a wave of superheated air, protecting his friends from the worst of the grenade's effects. As the wave dispersed, Stahn dared to peer round the robot's bulk. A heap of bodies lay further up the corridor, their limbs twisted and scorched.

'There'll be others,' he warned, checking the charge in his gun. 'How are you doing, Clarence?'

Behind him, the chimpanzee had ripped the cover from the keypad on the wall. 'It's a bit more difficult than I expected,' Clarence called back. 'It's a variable lock. It could literally be any number at any given time. A revolving combination of infinite variations.'

'Well, you've only got a finite time to crack it!' Vern called back. She could already hear the echo of approaching Zargon boots.

Reaching inside his tunic, Clarence pulled out a tiny leather pouch. Snapping it open, he let his fingers wander over a collection of small precision tools. 'Nope, nope, nope,' he mumbled as he rejected each in turn. 'Aha!' he exclaimed at last, pulling an OmniKey from the pouch. 'First things first,' he muttered. Applying the key to the intricate circuitry in the keypad, he toggled a switch on its slender stem. Soon, a reading appeared on a small screen. 'Hmm,' Clarence mused. 'It's cycling through a Fibonacci series.' His thoughts were interrupted by a chunk of masonry embedding itself in the wall beside him.

'We've got company!' Stahn shouted back.

'I'd noticed,' Clarence shot back, archly. He could just make out a new contingent of guards, advancing through the smoke. Once again, the air was thick with ice bullets.

'I'm sure how long we can hold them!' Vern called in desperation. She had noticed that even Rudy was beginning to wilt beneath the onslaught.

'Don't worry,' Clarence yelled. 'I've almost got it.' He turned his attention back to the keypad. 'If it's a Fibonacci series, all I have to do is stop the sequence and determine its current value.' Selecting another tool from his pouch, he pressed it carefully to the keypad's logic circuits. Attaching the OmniKey, another series of numbers appeared on the screen. At first, they were a blur. Within moments, however, they had slowed. Soon, it had settled on a single three digit number. Three, seven, seven. 'Got it!' Clarence yelled in excitement. 'Now, let's see if I remember my first year's mathematics training.' Snapping the cover shut, he input a sequence of numbers. 'Six, one, zero. Nine, eight, seven.'

'Clarence!' Vern and Stahn were being forced back towards him. Rudy was staggering unsteadily beneath a hail of HE Gun fire.

'One moment!' Clarence yelled back, impatiently. 'One, five, nine, seven. Two, five, eight, four. Four, one, eight, one.'

He could barely believe it himself when, with a hiss, the door slid open. 'I'm through!' he called back to his companions and soon Vern and Stahn were following him into the control room, their guns blazing as they retreated. Last of all, came Rudy. He was large enough to wedge himself in the door, his broad back, arms and legs acting as a barricade against the ice bullets.

'How long can you hold 'em, Rudy?' Clarence asked.

'As long as you need,' the robot boomed above the din.

Placing their guns on a console, the two scientists ran to the gravity well controls. Flicking a switch, Stahn brought up a live picture on a monitor. It showed a quiet region of space, its stars shimmering gently in the stillness of the void. He reached inside his uniform to pull out a key on a chain, nodding earnestly as Vern did the same. Reaching out in unison, they inserted their keys into identical ports and, on a count of three, turned them.

XVIII
UP ABOVE

'**H**ow the hell did they get in?' Grand Leutna Shavan stared at her subordinate, daring him to answer. Behind her, a picture of the control room was playing. She had watched as, a thousand metres below, the scientists had gained entry to the control room. She had recognised the talking chimpanzee and giant robot as associates of John Lovell.

'We're still trying to ascertain the details.' Leutna Krahl was trembling as he spoke. 'All we know is that they didn't use the usual entrances.'

Shavan was apoplectic. 'Of course they didn't use the usual entrances. That's the point of infiltration!' She thumped her hand down on a table top, smashing its glass surface into a hundred tiny cracks. 'Incompetence everywhere!' she bellowed, barely in control of her emotions. 'Jaht, Mev, Dravit, now this.' She marched right up to her subordinate. 'If they've got into the control room, we can assume the device has been compromised. Where's our nearest base to those coordinates!'

Leutna Krahl stabbed at a portable computer pad. 'We have a small attack force on exercises in the Cobalt Belt.'

'Send them in, just to be sure.'

'Yes, ma'am,' the Leutna nodded.

'Get into that control room. If Lovell isn't with them, find him.'

Krahl snapped his heels together in acknowledgment of the order.

'If he's not on the home world,' the Grand Leutna continued, 'get his whereabouts from his friends. By any means necessary.'

'They did it!' Colonel Zana was staring through the cockpit windshield. There, just off The Valiant's port bow, the universe itself seemed alive, flexing and bending as if struggling to take a physical form. 'The gravity well has been disengaged.'

Ro, Jhy and Lovell craned their necks to watch as the stars shimmered and blurred. Impossibly, the light was coalescing into a solid structure. Suddenly, they were confronted by the Doomsday Device. It hung in space, majestic and monstrous in equal degree. Lovell couldn't help but gasp at its sheer size.

'How did they build that?' he whispered.

'From what the scientists told us,' Zana replied, sadly, 'at great cost to their own home world.'

'Now what?' Ro asked. 'You got a plan, right?'

Lovell smiled. 'Oh, we got a plan.' He looked at Jhy and the robot dog nestling in his lap. 'Dash?' he called, pointing through the glass to the space station beyond. 'Go get it, boy!'

The little dog yapped in response, its tail wagging furiously with excitement. Jhy held him up and looked into his visual sensors. 'Dash?' he began. 'You know what to do. Get to that duct and get out as soon as the job's done.' He tickled the robot's mechanical ears. 'And be careful.'

'Valiant,' came Clarence's voice from the comms. 'Can you hear me?'

Lovell leaned over. 'Go ahead,' he snapped as he held his finger on the button.

'We've disengaged the gravity well,' Clarence reported back. 'You've got a few minutes before we engage the plasma cannon. We've attracted a lot of interest, so I'm not sure how long we can wait.'

'Roger that,' Lovell replied. 'We're sending Dash out right now. He's heading straight for those vents.'

Dash's mini thrusters blazed as he crossed the short distance to the device. As he drew nearer, its size became even more apparent. The diminutive robot seemed like a grain of sand on a beach in comparison. He felt the pull of its gravity as he approached and switched to vertical thrust to slow his descent, landing on the smooth metal hull with a *clang*. Adjusting his visual sensors, he located the vents ahead of him. As he approached the hatches, his nose twitched. He could sense the latent energy in the plasma beneath. He knew that, once the duct had been blocked, that energy would be released. His robotic brain had calculated that he would have just six minutes to traverse the five kilometres back to the surface before the plasma erupted. It would be tight. Dash wagged his tail, happy to be of use to his masters. Skidding to a halt by the vent, he paused to look into the chasm beneath.

'Woah!' Lovell stepped forward to prevent Jhy tipping forward.

'That's a long way down,' Jhy exclaimed, his eyes tight shut. Through his psychic connection with Dash, he could see the vent stretching down into the bowels of the device.

'It's okay,' soothed Colonel Zana. 'Let him go. He'll be safe.'

Jhy nodded. 'Okay, Dash,' he whispered. 'Let's go.'

Through his mind's eye, he saw the dog tip over the edge of the vent. There was barely enough room even for his tiny body. Jhy felt himself tightening his shoulders, such was the strength of his connection.

'I can't see where you're going, boy,' he muttered. 'Give me some light.'

Lovell looked on as Dash and, by extension Jhy, continued his journey down.

Colonel Zana turned to track his descent on a monitor. 'He's half a kilometre down,' she announced.

'So, he sees what the dog sees?' Ro was bemused.

Lovell smiled. 'Sees, feels *and* hears,' he said. 'They're practically joined at the hip.'

'Wild.' Ro looked impressed. 'Where did you find these guys?' she asked with a glance to Zana.

'It's a long story,' Lovell replied, cryptically. 'In fact, it's *several* long stories.'

'What do they see in you?' Ro teased.

'Aside from my rugged good looks, you mean?' Lovell shot back with a wink.

Ro leaned forward, suddenly serious. 'Threep thought the world of you, you know.'

Lovell nodded. 'And I thought the world of Threep.' He looked sombre. 'Ro, if I get through this, I'm gonna find out who really killed him.'

Ro shrugged. 'I tried that. But the trail gets cold pretty quick.'

'I'd start by finding out who doctored that video to put me at the scene.'

Ro was suspiciously silent.

'You?' Lovell gasped. 'You altered the security video?'

'I had to,' Ro pleaded. 'The Galactic Court insisted they needed evidence.'

'Wow.' Lovell wasn't sure what to think. 'Now I've heard it all.'

'You'll never understand what I've been through since Threep was killed.' Ro's eyes filled with tears. Lovell couldn't be certain if they were genuine. 'If there was another way, I would've taken it.'

'There's *always* another way,' Lovell hissed.

'Okay, so I'll make it up to you one day.' Ro folded her arms and moved to gaze out of the cockpit windshield. 'Since when did you get to be so honourable?'

Colonel Zana was doing her best to ignore the argument. 'As much as I hate to intrude on private grief,' she began, carefully, 'I think we might have company.'

Lovell sprang to his feet to join her by the monitor. Sure enough, a pattern of three dots had appeared, moving at speed towards their current position.

'I've got visual,' Ro confirmed, pointing through the glass.

Lovell turned back to Jhy. 'How's Dash doing?'

'He's doing the best he can,' the boy replied. 'In fact, the gravity is increasing as he falls. If anything, he's getting faster.'

Lovell reached over to switch on the comms. 'Clarence,' he barked, 'how are you holding up?'

'We're sitting pretty for now,' came the response from the Zargon home world, 'but they're throwing everything at us, and all we've got between them and us is Rudy.'

Lovell nodded, grimly. He could hear the ricochet of ice bullets on metal as Clarence spoke. 'Tell him to stand firm.'

'He's doing the best he can, but we're gonna have to activate the plasma coils and get outta here pretty soon.'

'Understood,' Lovell replied, sweat pricking on his forehead. He stole a glance at the monitor showing Dash's position. 'We're just minutes away from collapsing that duct.'

'We can give you minutes,' came Clarence's response, 'but not many.'

Lovell clicked the comms off. 'Jhy, we need to be as quick as we can.'

Before Jhy could reply, The Valiant was rocked by a series of nearby explosions.

'It's those ships,' Ro called, peering through the glass. 'They're Zargon. And they don't seem too pleased to see us.'

Zana toggled a switch on her monitor to see a live feed from the device's surface. It showed that two of the ships had landed on its surface and were letting down their ramps. Two teams of Zargon soldiers were making their way to the vents.

'How did they know?' Lovell asked.

Zana's fingers danced over the keyboard. She thumped her fist against the dashboard in exasperation. 'They've been monitoring Clarence's transmissions from the home world.'

Lovell sprang for a locker in a nearby bulkhead. 'Ro, you and me have got to get down there and protect Dash.' Another blast rocked the ship. 'Zana, you stay here and take care of Jhy.' He pointed through the windshield. 'And that other ship.'

He reached into the locker and threw a suit and helmet to Ro. 'Suit up,' he panted, 'then start your hopper.'

Within minutes, Ro was fighting with her little ship's controls as she rode the wave from another nearby explosion. 'They're getting frisky!' she called. 'You okay to find a spot to set down? I got my hands full.'

'Sure.' Lovell could feel every bump and jolt from the blast. 'You didn't think to fit dampeners on this thing?'

'Dampeners are for wimps,' Ro teased from the pilot's seat. 'If it can keep up with your ion engines it can stand a little laser flak.'

Lovell sighed as the cramped cabin shook again. 'There,' he said, pointing at a small monitor. 'Put us down on the other side of those vents. That pylon will give us cover as we land.'

'Will do,' said Ro, breezily. 'Partner.'

Lovell shook his head. She was enjoying this *way* too much.

With a sudden change of course, Ro overshot the pylon then swung the hopper round a full hundred and eighty degrees. Reaching across the dashboard, she extended the landing gear and cut the main engines. 'Hang on to your hat.'

Despite wearing a full space suit and helmet, Lovell instinctively reached for the brim of his hat only to remember he had left it on The Valiant.

'Oh, Lovell,' Ro laughed. 'You are priceless.'

Lovell felt his stomach turn as the hopper dropped like a stone. 'We don't have time for landing thrusters,' Ro explained.

'Don't tell me,' Lovell gulped. 'Thrusters are for wimps.'

The hopper slammed into the surface of the device. Even before it had settled, Ro was on her feet. She planted her fist into the door control and the hatch hissed open. 'Last one out's a Lanta egg,' she smiled as she cocked her rifle. She had stepped from the ship even before Lovell had had a chance to unclip his restraints. He could already hear laser fire. Ro was clearly giving them hell.

'Hey, Lovell,' came Ro's voice over his helmet comms. 'Coming to join the party?'

Lovell cocked his own rifle and stepped through the hatch.

The first thing he noticed was the gravity. Due to its mass, the Doomsday Device was generating its own gravitational pull. It felt a little bouncy, but Lovell found he could propel himself to Ro's position with a kick of his feet. She was crouching behind the pylon, her gun trained on a line of Zargon soldiers beyond the vent.

'I'm counting a dozen of them,' she said as she let off a volley from her rifle.

'I'm not sure I like those odds,' Lovell retorted as he squatted beside her. Looking out, he could see lines of infantry making their way to the vents. They marched in tight groups of three or four, their HE Guns spitting bullets of ice. Lovell could hear them thwacking into the pylon above him, showering him with tiny shards of frozen water.

'One of those could rip your arm off,' he cautioned.

Ro lay on her belly. 'Best not let that happen, then,' she smiled. 'Cover me.' Lifting herself onto her elbows and knees, she made her way slowly to a gully on the surface. Lovell fired over her head, clipping two soldiers, one in the head and one in the stomach. They clutched at their wounds as they fell. Lovell could see the air escaping from the holes in their suits.

'Dash is a kilometre away,' Jhy reported over comms. 'You have to buy him time.'

'We're doing just that, kid,' Lovell replied, felling another Zargon with a shot from his rifle. 'Let us know when he's at that duct.'

The comms clicked and Lovell heard Clarence's voice. 'Lovell, Rudy's struggling to hold them. We gotta blow this thing.'

'We're almost there,' Lovell hissed. 'Dash is moments away.'

'Moments is all we got,' came Clarence's response. Lovell could hear the desperation in his voice. 'Rudy's holding up but they're blasting the wall around him. If they get in…'

'I hear ya,' Lovell breathed. The comms clicked off.

Ro had found a new position, crouched in a small depression in the metal. Squinting through her rifle's sights, she loosed a barrage of laser fire, mowing down three more of the advancing Zargons.

'Lovell!' came Zana's voice from The Valiant. 'They're bringing in reinforcements!'

Just as the comms snapped off, a huge explosion tore through the air, throwing Lovell off his feet. He fought for breath as he landed, winded, in an ungainly heap.

'You okay, Lovell?'

He looked up to see Ro peering over a newly gouged scar in the metal landscape. It was all he could do to raise his hand in acknowledgement. Ro pointed up into the sky, and Lovell saw the third Zargon ship turning to make another pass. The Valiant was on its tail, its laser cannon blazing.

'I daren't fire at him when he gets too close,' cried Zana over comms. 'If I miss him, I hit you.'

Lovell found his voice at last. 'Do what you can,' he panted. He struggled to his knees and tried to focus on the approaching forces. He saw Ro was just metres from the vent. On the other side, a Zargon soldier was reaching from his belt. Lovell knew that could mean only one thing. 'Light grenade!' he yelled as he levelled his rifle. He saw Ro look up as he fired. The soldier fell to the ground as Lovell's shot found its mark. But it was too late. In the weaker gravity, the grenade seemed to arc lazily towards the vent. Lovell guessed the soldier had set the timer to explode deep in the bowels of the device. The deeper it fell, the quicker it would travel. Dash would be destroyed in the blast and the plan would fail. Following his gaze, Ro saw the grenade falling towards the vent. Launching herself with a kick, she propelled herself in its direction, her rifle spewing laser fire before her.

'Ro!' called Lovell. 'If you touch that, you'll trip its safety trigger!' But he knew that the alternative was worse. He watched, helpless, as Ro snatched at the grenade, plucking it from its trajectory to the vent. Clutching it to her chest, she slammed into the ground and rolled, her legs kicking frantically behind her. Now she had a hold of the grenade she had to get rid of it, but her momentum prevented her stretching out her hands to release it. Instead, she barrelled into a group of panicking soldiers, sending them scattering like a cosmic game of ninepins. And then the grenade exploded.

A flash of light cast strange shadows on the ground as a great ball of heat scorched everything within its reach. Ro and the nearest soldiers were caught in the blast and sent reeling into space.

Lovell watched in shock. He barely heard Jhy over his helmet comms. 'Dash is in position,' the boy cried, excitedly. 'He's collapsing the duct!'

'We're engaging the plasma coils,' came Clarence's response from the home world, 'and getting the hell outta here. I suggest you do the same.'

Lovell shook his head to clear it. 'Uh, sure,' he replied. He watched as Ro's lifeless body fell back to the ground, her space suit smouldering.

'And be quick, Lovell,' added Zana from The Valiant. 'The cavalry's coming back for another piece of you.'

Lovell looked up to see the Zargon ship closing on him at speed. He suddenly felt very exposed. 'Ro's dead,' he heard himself say.

There was a brief pause before the Colonel replied. 'Then she'd want you to save yourself.' The comms clicked off.

XIX

THE RETURN

Back on the home world, Vern threw the final switch in a sequence to activate the plasma coils. 'They've got minutes,' she said, turning to Clarence. The sound of alarms filled the air. 'And we've got to go. Every soldier on the planet will be here at any moment.'

Clarence nodded. 'Let's just hope Dash is on his way back to the surface.' On the monitor, he could see the device's huge claws beginning to deploy in response to the plasma coils' activation. It was a sight that made him shiver.

'We've done the easy part,' said Stahn. 'Now to get off this planet the same way we got in.'

'But the place will be crawling with soldiers,' Vern cried.

'Well, we can't stay here forever,' Stahn retorted.

Clarence noticed the rising panic in their voices. 'Okay, Rudy,' he snapped, patting the metal giant on his chest plate. 'Ready?'

Rudy nodded. 'Ready,' he confirmed. As the robot turned in the doorway and prepared himself to walk into a hail of gunfire, Clarence gasped. The metal casing on Rudy's back was buckled and scarred from defending the door. In places, Clarence could even see bare circuitry.

'We'll be as quick as we can,' Clarence assured him.

'Thank you,' Rudy rumbled.

With that, he leaned into the gunfire and started the journey back down the corridor towards the jagged hole in the ceiling. Stahn, Vern and Clarence peered around him with their weapons in hand, sending volley after volley of laser fire towards the approaching soldiers. They seemed to have little effect.

'This is so much worse than before!' Stahn yelled. 'Their numbers are so much greater.'

'Don't you dare say we don't stand a chance,' Clarence admonished him. 'We've come this far, we can't give up now.'

Rudy's pace had slowed beneath the onslaught. Sheets of flame washed over him as the advancing Zargons reversed their HE Guns. In the midst of the fireball, waves of bullets fell like nails, embedding themselves in Rudy's armour.

'He's failing!' Vern called above the noise.

'Rudy never fails!' Clarence shouted back, although he didn't sound so certain.

Leaning around the great robot's waist, he took pot-shots through the smoke. Three soldiers dropped where they stood, only to be trampled over as their comrades pushed forward.

'Clarence!' Vern's cry forced the chimp to glance back. There he saw Stahn, a surprised look on his face. 'He's been shot,' Vern was whimpering. Looking down, Clarence saw the scientist's uniform was stained with blood. He was clutching at a wound in his stomach, his mouth moving silently in shock.

'I'll take him!' Clarence yelled. 'You take his gun!' Moving as swiftly as he could, the chimp lifted Stahn carefully under the arms and swung him over his shoulders.

'Incoming!'

Clarence's heart sank. Vern was pointing fearfully down the corridor where a barrage of light grenades was swinging through the smoke. Even with Rudy as a barricade, they were finished. 'Get back to the control room!' Clarence shouted. 'It's our only chance!' He saw a look of defeat in Vern's eyes. She knew it was over. Clarence relaxed. He knew she was right. Lowering Stahn gently to the floor, he pulled Vern towards him and placed a hand over her eyes, waiting for the end.

But the end didn't come. At least, not the way Clarence had expected. Time seemed to slow. Rudy gave a mighty roar as a figure seemed to resolve itself out of thin air, a protective dome of energy emanating from his outstretched palms. Clarence, Vern and the injured Stahn were bathed in a blue-green glow. Daring to look up, Clarence saw the light grenades explode as they made contact with the energy shield. The power of the blast was absorbed entirely. There was no flash of light or ball of heat, just a faint glow as the energy was absorbed and dissipated.

'What's going on?' Vern asked, her eyes wide with fear. 'What's Rudy doing?'

'You know,' Clarence mused, gnawing his lip as he thought, 'I'm not a hundred percent sure it *is* Rudy.'

With the last Zargon soldier incapacitated, Lovell turned back to Ro's hopper. He considered retrieving her body, but noticed the Zargon ship turning back for another pass. Suddenly, the sky was ablaze with laser fire. The metal ground splintered into sparks all around him. He could feel the heat through his space suit.

'That was close,' Lovell muttered.

'I'm on his tail,' came Colonel Zana's voice from The Valiant, 'but you've got to get off of that thing before it blows. Jhy says Dash is on his way out but it's gonna be close.'

Frankly, Lovell had more to think about than the survival chances of a little metal dog. The hopper was now just metres away. He kicked at the ground for a final leap, only to see a flash of brilliant light above him. The Zargon ship released a barrage of laser fire that fell all around him. Lovell was thrown off his feet, twisting into the air before crashing to the ground. For a while, there was only darkness. When he finally found the strength to open his eyes, he found he was looking directly skywards. The Zargon ship was trailing smoke from one of its aft engines, clearly the result of a direct hit from The Valiant. In a last, desperate attempt to finish Lovell off for good, it was raking the ground with scorching laser fire.

Lovell rose unsteadily to his feet as the wall of destruction approached. He realised he was out of time. Raising his hands to shield his eyes against the glare, he made peace with the Universe and promised it that, next time around, he wouldn't be such a klutz. A thousand faces flashed before his eyes, people he had known and loved. People he had killed. And then he realised he had had far too much time. Surely, he should have been dead by now. He peered carefully through his fingers and gasped. There before him stood a man. He had a bald head and wore simple robes. His hands were raised above his head, radiating a protective dome of fizzing energy over Lovell's head. The ship's lasers were absorbed with little more than a flicker.

'To a mind that is still, the whole universe surrenders.'

Lovell recognised the voice at once. Somehow, he could hear it echoing through his very bones. 'Sumara,' he breathed. 'But how?'

'I am both here and not here,' the mystic replied, though his lips didn't move at all.

Lovell tapped his helmet to snap on his comms. 'Clarence,' he panted. 'It's Sumara. He's here.'

'He's here too, Lovell,' came Clarence's elated response. 'Or at least, I think he is. Rudy's projecting a power that I've never seen before. It's protecting us while we get back to the ship. Bullets, grenades, everything's just bouncing off.'

'John Lovell,' came Sumara's voice again. 'Doubt is good, but sometimes faith is better.'

Lovell snapped off the comms. Sumara was right. He had to trust his old friend would protect him on his way back to Ro's hopper. With the Zargon ship's laser fire dissipating harmlessly on Sumara's energy field, Lovell made a final effort to propel himself up the ramp and through the hopper's hatch. Once inside, he punched the door control and threw himself into the pilot's seat, stabbing at the controls on the dashboard with a frantic speed.

'Fuel mix... thrusters,' he muttered as he familiarised himself with the controls. 'Ha! Dampeners! I knew it!'

He threw back the controls and the hopper rose gracefully into the air. Looking back through the cockpit window, he saw the Zargon ship slam into the Doomsday Device. Within moments it had erupted into a mass of burning, twisted metal. Beyond it, Lovell saw Sumara lowering his arms. As the hopper lifted away, his final view was of the mystic's form seeming to lose integrity. Finally, he drifted away like smoke on the wind.

'Thanks, old friend,' Lovell whispered, then he turned his hopper to rendezvous with The Valiant.

'Let's get outta here!' Lovell yelled as he sprinted through the hatch onto the Kestran ship.

Colonel Zana was at the dashboard, her fingers dancing over the controls. 'We've got to wait,' she said.

Lovell was aghast. 'What?' he boomed. 'We've got just moments until that thing blows!'

'Then we have moments to wait,' Zana replied, gently. She nodded towards the co-pilot's chair. There sat Jhy, his face wet with tears.

'We have to wait for Dash,' he sobbed. 'Or he will die in the blast.'

Lovell softened. 'Of course we have, kid.' He looked at Zana, mindful of just how little time they might have left. 'But he would want you to be – '

'There he is!' Jhy screamed, pointing through the windshield. Sure enough Lovell could see the little robot dog tearing through the vent hatches, his mini thrusters burning bright behind him.

'Let's go get the dog,' Lovell snapped. Zana leaned against the controls, stabbing at a button to open the airlock doors. She could already see the Doomsday Device was aglow with a build up of plasma. With the ventilation duct destroyed, the superheated coolant had nowhere to go but backwards. She didn't want to be anywhere near it when it blew.

'We're clear of the home world,' cried Clarence over the comms, 'and heading for Kestra.'

Lovell jammed his hat on his head and straightened the brim. 'On that heap of junk?' he laughed. 'We'll come and get you.'

With Dash safely recovered, The Valiant slipped silently into hyperspace, its ion engines burning bright as the stars in the sky. Behind it, the Doomsday Device seemed to hang expectantly in the void. Then, fighting to contain the internal pressure, its metal surface buckled and flexed. Finally, it relented. The plasma erupted in a frenzy of heat and light. Its metal hull melted in a moment, releasing a sun's worth of energy in nanoseconds. The Doomsday Device collapsed in on itself and cracked apart, its huge metal claws spinning away into space. The shock wave spiralled out and away, carrying the debris towards the Kestran sun. There it was destined to twist and turn for eternity, reflecting the light into the night sky like new stars, forever warning of the Zargons' folly.

Grand Leutna Shavan slammed her fist against the windowpane. If it hadn't been made of toughened glass, she was sure she would have thrown the Leutna through it. He stood behind her, trembling.

'It was destroyed, ma'am,' Feng stuttered. 'Utterly and completely.'

Shavan bit her lip. 'And the invaders?'

'Escaped, ma'am.' The Leutna swallowed. 'We have indications that two of the traitor scientists were among them.'

'The scientists that I sent Under-Leutna Mev to kill?' Shavan spat.

'Yes, ma'am.'

The Grand Leutna was unnervingly quiet.

Her subordinate cleared his throat, self-consciously. 'We have reason to believe John Lovell was on the device, ma'am.'

There was another silence then, quite suddenly, Shavan threw back her head and laughed.

'Of course he was!' she wailed. 'Who else could it have been? The Zargon Empire's very own thorn in the side.'

'It appears he had help,' Leutna Feng continued, bravely. 'From friends. The first was Ro Silvari, the woman who appeared to be on our side.'

'Anyone else?' The Grand Leutna shook her head in despair.

The Leutna faltered. 'Just before it crashed,' he stammered, 'our attack ship registered a spike in psychic energy both here on the home world and on the device.'

'Psychic energy?'

'It would seem Lovell had help from an associate that we thought dead. Visual scans identified him as a man called Sumara.'

Shavan bristled at the name. She had replayed the footage of the siege on the Zargon asteroid countless times. She had seen her brother battling with a man named Sumara in his private quarters. She flicked her eyes to the wall. There hung her brother's laser whip, the very weapon he had used to kill Sumara. She unclipped it gingerly from its peg and coiled it round her fingers. Someone would have to pay for the day's disappointments. Only then could she plan her next move. Turning to the table in the centre of the room, she flicked a switch.

Leutna Feng wore a look of terror as the blinds lowered over the windows, plunging the room into darkness. Eventually, all he could see was the crackling of energy along the length of the whip and the eerie smile of a woman who was about to enjoy herself far too much.

XX

THE FIVE STAR FIVE

The Kestran moons hung, pale and waxy, in the early evening sky. A stage had been erected in the presidential gardens, festooned with musical flowers and garlands of vivid blooms. A band played as the dignitaries took their seats. Lovell, Colonel Zana, Jhy, Rudy and Clarence were led out to their places. It was a perfect day. Lovell looked through the looba trees to where the capital city of Estoran nestled between gleaming mountains, its towers and spires piercing a bright blue sky.

Taking his seat near the stage, he saw Colonel Zana smiling back at him. She looked smart in her military uniform, her hair piled high on her head. With a wink, she turned away to engage in conversation with another military commander. Beside her, Lovell could see Clarence in his gleaming white tunic, waving to the crowd. No doubt he'd be signing autographs later. Next to the chimp sat a smiling Jhy, his pet dog on his lap. Dash had suffered no more than a few scorch marks as a result of his adventures. The Kestran engineers had seen to it that he looked as good as new for the ceremony. Finally, Rudy stood at the end of the row, his newly polished armour shining in the sunlight. Lovell smiled. He scrubbed up well for a demolition robot. Rudy seemed to sense he was being watched. Turning his great head, he noticed Lovell and gave a small bow. Lovell frowned. Rudy was suddenly a much more enigmatic figure. He had refused to explain his newfound powers, beyond insisting that he was now more man than machine. Lovell couldn't argue with that. Somehow, Rudy had summoned up Sumara's spirit just when he had been needed most. If the mystic was somehow present within Rudy's metal frame, then he was a very special robot indeed.

A round of applause signified the end of the music. An announcement instructed the audience to stand and the Planetary

Anthem was played as the President took to the stage. He looked resplendent in his robes of office, his mane of jet-black hair falling over his shoulders. He took his place at a podium and cleared his throat.

'Exceptional times produce exceptional people, and we are living through exceptional times.' There was a murmur of agreement from the assembled dignitaries. 'We find our very way of life under threat. A malevolent force wishes to destroy us. To them, our freedoms and prosperity are an affront, and they would take them from us if they could.' The President scanned the crowd with his steely eyes. 'But they never will!' There was a burst of spontaneous applause. The President waited for the hubbub to subside, then continued. 'The Zargons are products of their own fear. Their Elite Forces cling to power with an iron fist. Their own people are subjugated, dissent is not tolerated. But what they fear, we celebrate.' Another smattering of applause. 'While they fear difference, we embrace it.' He nodded to where Vern was sitting, alone, in the crowd. There was much muttering of approval and Vern's neighbour reached out to squeeze her shoulder. 'In Kestra's hour of need,' the President continued, 'five particular individuals stood up to be counted, and only one was Kestran. We are proud that our humble planet inspires those from other worlds. We are proud to open our arms to people of all races. We are proud that they would fight beside us.'

At this, the audience took to their feet and applauded again. Lovell was embarrassed at the ovation, but felt duty bound to nod and smile in response.

'These exceptional times,' continued the President as the noise died away, 'have thrown up new heroes, although I know they would blush at the word.' There was much nodding of heads. 'Five individuals who, today, we award with the Kestran Stars.' The President held up a medal comprising a row of glittering gold stars. 'These five stars represent the values upon which our society is built; freedom, equality, tolerance, diversity and dignity. I cannot think of anyone who better personifies those principles, than the five individuals before me. And so, I invite them to the stage to receive their commendations.'

A triumphant anthem accompanied Lovell and his companions to the stage where they stood for a moment, acknowledging the thunderous applause.

And then a shot rang out.

At first, there was confusion. The applause continued for a while as the crowd looked about them for the source of the noise, then someone screamed. Lovell saw the President slump onto the podium and slide to the floor. A slick of blood oozed from a wound in his head. Colonel Zana sprinted to the President's side.

Someone shouted, 'Call a medic! The President's been shot!'

Several people in the crowd had started crying. Fearful of more gunfire, others ducked behind their chairs or even attempted to leave the auditorium. Kneeling beside the President, Colonel Zana placed a finger on his neck to feel for a pulse. As she strained to feel for any signs of life, she saw the President's lips move. Zana put her ear to his mouth.

'Pulse,' the President gasped. 'Project... Pulse.' His last breath escaped with a horrible rattle, and his head rolled to one side.

'Make some room!' shouted Lovell as he ran to Zana's side. A small crowd had suddenly gathered around him. 'Give the President some air!'

'There's no need,' Zana said quietly, a look of shock on her face. 'The President is dead.'

OTHER GREAT TITLES
BY ANDERSON ENTERTAINMENT

available from
shop.gerryanderson.com

Five Star Five: John Lovell and the Zargon Threat

THE TIME: THE FUTURE
THE PLACE: THE UNIVERSE

The peaceful planet of Kestra is under threat. The evil Zargon forces are preparing to launch a devastating attack from an asteroid fortress. With the whole Kestran system in the Zargons' sights, Colonel Zana looks to one man to save them. Except one man isn't enough. Gathering a crack team around him including a talking chimpanzee, a marauding robot and a mystic monk, John Lovell must infiltrate the enemy base and save Kestra from the Zargons!

STINGRAY

Stingray: Operation Icecap

The Stingray crew discover an ancient diving bell that leads them on an expeditionary voyage through the freezing waters of Antarctica to the land of a lost civilisation. Close on the heels of Troy Tempest and the pride of the World Aquanaut Security Patrol is the evil undersea ruler Titan. Ahead of them are strange creatures who inhabit underground waterways and an otherworldly force with hidden powers strong enough to overwhelm even Stingray's defences.

Stingray: Monster from the Deep

Commander Shore's old enemy, Conrad Hagen, is out of prison and back on the loose with his beautiful but devious daughter, Helga. When they hijack a World Aquanaut Security Patrol vessel and kidnap Atlanta, it's up to Captain Troy Tempest and the crew of Stingray to save her. But first they will have to uncover the mystery of the treasure of Sanito Cathedral and escape the fury of the monster from the deep.

Intergalactic Rescue 4: Stellar Patrol

It is the 22nd century. The League of Planets has tasked Jason Stone, Anne Warran and their two robots, Alpha and Zeta to explore the galaxy, bringing hope to those in need of rescue.

On board Intergalactic Rescue 4, they travel to ice moons and jungle planets in 10 exciting adventures that see them journey further across the stars than anyone before.

But what are the secret transmissions that Anne discovers?

And why do their rescues seem to be taking them on a predetermined course?

Soon, Anne discovers that her co-pilot, Jason, might be on a quest of his own…

A GERRY ANDERSON PRODUCTION

THUNDERBIRDS

Thunderbirds: Operation Asteroids

What starts out as a simple rescue mission to save a trapped miner on the moon, soon turns out to be one of International Rescue's greatest catastrophes. After the Hood takes members of International Rescue hostage during the rescue, a chase across space and an altercation among the asteroids only worsens the situation.

With the Hood hijacking Thunderbird Three along with Brains, Lady Penelope and Tin-Tin, it is up to the Tracy brothers to stage a daring rescue in the mountain tops of his hidden lair.

But can they rescue Brains before his engineering genius is used for the destructive forces of evil?

Thunderbirds: Terror from the Stars

Thunderbird Five is attacked by an unknown enemy with uncanny powers. An unidentified object is tracked landing in the Gobi desert, but what's the connection? Scott Tracy races to the scene in the incredible Thunderbird One, but he cannot begin to imagine the terrible danger he is about to encounter.

Alone in the barren wilderness, he is possessed by a malevolent intelligence and assigned a fiendish mission – one which, if successful, will have the most terrifying consequences for the entire world.

International Rescue are about to face their most astounding adventure yet!

Thunderbirds: Peril in Peru

An early warning of disaster brings International Rescue to Peru to assist in relief efforts following a series of earth tremors – and sends the Thunderbirds in search of an ancient Inca treasure trove hidden beneath a long-lost temple deep in the South American jungle!

When Lady Penelope is kidnapped by sinister treasure hunters, Scott Tracy and Parker are soon hot on their trail.

Along the way they'll have to solve a centuries-old mystery, brave the inhospitable wilderness of the jungle and even tangle with a lost tribe – with the evil Hood close behind them all the way…

SPACE: 1999 Maybe There –
The Lost Stories from SPACE: 1999

Strap into your Moon Ship and prepare for a trip to an alternate universe! Gathered here for the first time are the original stories written in the early days of production on the internationally acclaimed television series SPACE: 1999. Uncover the differences between Gerry and Sylvia Anderson's original story Zero G, George Bellak's first draft of The Void Ahead and Christopher Penfold's uncredited shooting script Turning Point. Each of these tales shows the evolution of the pilot episode with scenes and characters that never made it to the screen. Wonder at a tale that was NEVER filmed where the Alpha People, desperate to migrate to a new home, instigate a conflict between two alien races. Also included are Christopher Penfold's original storylines for Guardian of Piri and Dragon's Domain, an adaption of Keith Miles's early draft for All That Glisters and read how Art Wallace (Dark Shadows) originally envisioned the episode that became Matter of Life and Death. Discover how SPACE: 1999 might have been had they gone 'Maybe There?'